Walk
Beside Me,
Be My
Friend

Walk Beside Me, Be My Friend

JOAN OPPENHEIMER

SCHOLASTIC BOOK SERVICES

New York Toronto London Auckland Sydney Tokyo

Copyright © 1978 by Joan Oppenheimer. All rights reserved. Published by Scholastic Book Services, a division of Scholastic Magazine, Inc.
division of Scholastic Magazines, Inc.

12 11 10 9 8 7 6 5 4 3 2 1   2   8 9/7 0 1 2 3/8

Chapter One

Kris Wilding liked the last class of the day best, though not for any of the obvious reasons. The fact that school dismissed with the three o'clock bell had nothing to do with the way she felt, nor was Spanish her favorite subject.

She had no special feeling for the teacher, either — not since the day she really bombed on a surprise quiz and Miss Garcia kept her after class for a few minutes.

"Kris, you look so — so tired lately," she said. "Is there something wrong?" She added delicately, "A problem at home, perhaps?"

Kris took a deep breath. "There are lots of problems at home." Her voice was wry. Then, for some crazy reason, maybe because she *was* so tired, she went on to check them off on her fingers. Given one bit of encouragement, she might have sat down to talk about them, too. She felt that low.

"My mother works the noon to nine shift at the Long Beach Inn. She's a waitress, and nobody wants those lousy hours, so it pays a little better. My dad walked out on us six years ago.

"What it means is, I'm supposed to keep the house clean and cook and baby-sit the other kids, and they're supposed to help. Well, they don't, and I can't make them. My mother comes home ready for a fight, anyway, so she doesn't even listen when I try to tell her what's going on."

She stopped, anger burning through her as she noted Miss Garcia's glance at the clock on the rear wall. Why had she wasted her breath? Worse, why had she exposed family matters that should have been kept private? Sounding off like that, saying it all wrong. She should have known it would look like she wanted sympathy, and all she needed — desperately needed — was for someone to help.

Why hadn't she kept her mouth shut? She felt a hot, prickling shame, as if she suddenly stood naked in the quiet classroom.

The teacher said at last in her low gentle voice, "Kris, why don't you make an appointment with your counselor? Mrs. Adams might be able to help. That's her job — "

It was not Miss Garcia's job. And she didn't

seem anxious to take on any extra-curricular work. Kris couldn't blame her for that. She knew all too well how it felt to have too many jobs, always too much to do.

She did not consult the counselor, and she never again mentioned her difficulties at home to Miss Garcia. Possibly grateful for that, her teacher stretched a point and gave her a low C in Spanish rather than the D she deserved.

Even that gesture didn't explain the warm, comfortable feeling Kris so often experienced during that class. She sat in the very last row in the corner, for one thing, and that was pure luck because Miss Garcia had arranged them alphabetically.

By chance, too, there were a couple of very pretty and popular girls in that class. Kris played a favorite game all period, watching either Linda or Gail, listening to their choice of words, observing every gesture.

Sometimes she managed to erase herself, even the sense of herself, so completely, that for moments at a time it was almost as though Kris Wilding vanished into the person of Gail Parkins or Linda Utterbach. For those brief moments, she knew what it was like to be beautiful, poised, happy, together.

She played the game first in grammar school, and she still enjoyed it, though she knew it now for a form of fantasy. She even realized why she found it necessary, accepting the probability that the other ordinary people in this world, maybe the losers as well, fantasized as much as she did.

Anyone sixteen years old and ordinary in every way would naturally be interested in watching the Lindas and Gails around them, she decided. Certainly there was nothing interesting in anyone like herself, small and shaped more like a boy than her own fourteen-year-old sister, Patsy.

Her best friend, Mindy Carter, always pointed out how lucky she was to have short, curly, dark hair, especially because she could cut it herself with a little help on the back.

"It always looks so great," Mindy insisted. "You don't know how lucky you are not to have to mess with bleaching or streaking or even those dumb rinses. And you've got such wonderful skin."

She laughed at that point and made a crack about Patsy's complexion problems. "Old Pats might trade what she's got up front with you in in a hurry, if she could get rid of her zits in the bargain."

They were walking home from school as Mindy made the observation.

Kris wrinkled her nose. "She won't get rid of them as long as she keeps eating so much junk. The greasier it is, the better she likes it. And if she'd *wash* her face more often — but you know Patsy. She never listens."

For a moment, she studied Mindy, vaguely aware that some of the things that irritated her about her sister were also true of her friend. Mindy devoured junk food with equal appetite, and it showed in her spotty complexion as well as her plump body.

She liked snug tee shirts with raunchy words or phrases written on the chest. The one she wore today, however, boasted a realistic picture of a fried egg across each breast, a joke in itself inasmuch as Mindy's measurements were awesome.

She wore skin-tight jeans, as well, and carried a pair of ragged tennies on top of her books. She never wore shoes outside school if she could help it.

Kris could see the picture clearly: Mindy's hair always in transition from a bleaching or streaking job, usually straggling in a growing-out haircut. It was never overly clean, either. Yet Kris forgave the flaws, ignoring them simply as a matter of loyalty.

There were a great many things that Mindy overlooked about her, after all. If her house looked like a herd of buffalo had just stampeded through it, thanks to her twin brothers, Mindy never noticed. Doubtless her own home looked worse, Mindy's mother being alcoholic and her father career Navy. It meant, in his case, that he was rarely home.

"Would you come home if you had a choice? To that? To her?" Mindy had said once, cynically but without real anger.

Kris found that hard to understand. She

couldn't remember a time in the last few years when she herself had not been angry. Occasionally she questioned her friend, curiously, hoping that there might be some secret she could learn to rid herself of that painful emotion.

But Mindy shrugged off her questions. "It just ain't worth all the hassle," she said indifferently. "I don't care about either of them, and they don't care about me. Simple as that. I guess I'm tighter with old Clip than anybody." She added hastily, "And you, of course."

Mindy was easy to talk to. More than that, she seemed to be the only person who ever listened to Kris. When things built up to the explosion point, she could always count on Mindy.

Mrs. Kelly next door was nice enough and a real lifesaver because she kept an extra key and watched the twins if they got home before anyone else did. But Mrs. Kelly talked incessantly, whether or not she had an audience. She even talked back to the television screen. There was always a background of voices and music in her tiny cluttered house. No, Mrs. Kelly never listened to anybody. It made Mindy Carter doubly important in Kris's life.

The minute she opened the front door that day and saw the littered living room, she felt the anger inside coming to a slow boil. Greg and Guy had been told three days ago to clean up the mess on the scarred cocktail table and the rug, pieces from the Monopoly game, a jigsaw puzzle, and a model airplane kit. Old apple cores and dirty dishes lay on another table and on the floor halfway under the big chair. Pajama tops were stuffed behind a couch cushion, socks and tennis shoes beneath one end of the table.

Kris sucked in her breath through clenched teeth. Last night, her mother had climbed all over her about it.

"Least you can do is keep the place picked up," she said. "It looks like a pigpen, and it's been like that for days."

Kris stared at her. "You never listen to anything I tell you, do you? I've been after the twins to clean up that mess since Sunday. I spent half a day at the laundromat and did all the shopping. Why should I have to do everything around the house, too? I didn't drag that junk in there — "

"I don't want to hear any more about it." Her mother made an impatient gesture and turned away. "I've got enough to worry me without you bearing tales every minute I'm home."

"Bearing tales!" Kris yelled, outraged. "You put everything on me, don't you? I'm supposed to do the cooking and the laundry and clean the house, even baby-sit those brats. And you sit back and say, 'They'll all help. Give them a job to do.'" Bitterly, she mimicked her mother's instructions. Her tone made up in sarcasm what it lacked in the irritation with which the orders had actually been issued.

"Sounds really great, huh? Simple. Well, I've got news for you, those three won't lift a finger around here. Do you yell at them? No, you climb on me."

It ended for once with her mother screaming at all of them about her own problems. She worked long hours at a lousy job. She worried about the bills. She never got enough rest. And her kids gave her nothing but trouble. She didn't get any peace and quiet even during the few hours she could spend at home. Why did she have to put up with all this *hassle*?

Patsy started to cry and went to put her arms around her mother. Jane Wilding was a small, wiry woman whom Kris closely resembled. Jane's second daughter at fourteen was almost as tall as she.

"We're sorry, Mom, honest we are. We know how tired you get. We'll do better from now on. Really we will."

Kris left the room, almost physically ill from the scene. Patsy could always be counted on to whine like a three-year-old, babying her mother, fussing over her. Mama's pet, Kris thought with disgust. No wonder she always got her way.

Looking at the living room, she thought, Greg and Guy must come next on the list. She could hear them yelling back in their bedroom, throwing something against the wall in a slow steady rhythm.

At ten, they always seemed to be yelling, at her or each other or at their friends who trooped in and out of the house in a wave of noise and feverish activity. The twins hated baths, bedtime, all vegetables, and anyone who tried to tell them what to do. They either ignored Kris or went out of their way to torment her.

"Monsters!" she said to Mindy. "I knew they'd leave it like that."

"You gonna clean it up?" Mindy clucked when she saw her nod. "You're nuts, you know that?"

"It isn't worth any more yelling and hollering." She led the way back to the kitchen, dumping her books on the table. "I get sick to my stomach when I get mad. Sometimes I go in and throw up."

"You're kidding!" Elbows propped on the table, Mindy rested her chin in one palm. She looked at Kris, her eyes curious.

Kris poured two glasses of milk and put cookies and apples in the middle of the table before she sat down. "I guess it's because I get so frustrated," she said. "Nothing ever changes around here unless it gets worse. I feel like I'm beating my head against a wall, and it's never going to give way. The only thing that'll happen is — my head'll get hurt."

Mindy chewed for a moment, looking thoughtful. "Ever occur to you, your mother's set you up?" she said. "I mean, you're the heavy around here. You take all the guff from Patsy and the creeps back there, and you end up doing all the work."

"That's for sure," Kris muttered.

"She's smart." Mindy drank, set the empty glass down. "All your mother wants is peace and quiet. She knows what's going on. She just doesn't care. Unreal."

She shook her head. "Listen, when Clip and I get ready to split, you better come along. You're crazy if you put up with this routine any longer."

Kris shrugged. She got up, moving her apple and milk to the kitchen counter. Then she rummaged in the bin for potatoes and carrots and began to peel them at the sink.

Somehow, she couldn't see that Mindy would be much better off if she did follow through on her plans to run away. For one thing, Kris disliked Clip Franklin. Thinking about him, she felt a small chill on the back of her neck. She knew he didn't like her, either, the way his narrow black eyes laughed at her.

"I sure like that blouse," Mindy said into the short silence. "Pink's good on you, makes your skin look really great."

"Thanks." Kris turned to smile at her.

Mindy had always loved the long-sleeved pink blouse. She had hinted once about wanting to borrow it, but Kris hadn't picked up on it. The blouse would be skin tight on Mindy, which was the way she liked her clothes to fit.

But if Mindy wore it, Kris was afraid the blouse might get ripped or come back to her minus one of the buttons or, worse, stained from perspiration. She felt a little guilty, but still she had never offered to lend the blouse to Mindy.

She said now, changing the subject, "When are you and Clip leaving?"

"Last of June," Mindy said. "He's got a little money coming then." She stretched lazily and added in a soft croon, "Man, I can hardly wait. Nobody bugging me about nothing, never no more."

Kris turned to look at her. "I'll miss you," she said. "I just don't know what I'll do without you to talk to, Mindy."

Her friend said easily, "Better come along then."

"No." Kris stared down at the potato peeler in her hand, turning it from side to side as if she had never seen it before.

"No, I just can't see running away. Sure, I'd get rid of the things around here that drive me crazy, but — the whole idea scares me. You know? Where would I go? What would I do?"

"That's what's good about going off *with* somebody," Mindy said. "Well, you got a couple weeks to think about it. Every time you get so mad you throw up, you better think hard."

Kris sighed and picked up another potato. "I will," she said and nodded to herself. "I'll think about it."

Chapter
Two

Mindy went home about five. When Kris closed the door behind her, she went to pick up the living room, carrying the dirty dishes to the kitchen. Everything else she dumped in a cardboard box and took it back to the twins' room.

Greg's dark eyes narrowed when he saw it. "You dummy!" he said crossly. "If you lost any pieces, I'm gonna punch you a good one."

Kris did not reply. She retrieved more dishes from the top of the boys' battered chest of drawers and withdrew. There were three more glasses on the bathroom windowsill.

As she brushed by, Patsy turned from the

mirror, frowning. There were three angry blotches on one cheek, and she dabbed at another one on her chin with a piece of tissue.

She wore her hair long, well below her plump shoulders. In the harsh light from the ceiling bulb, the crown on her head shone with oil. It looked as if she were wearing a skull cap slightly darker than the rest of her hair.

"There you go." Her tone was accusing. "You scour the whole house for dishes when it's my turn to wash." She pointed at the stack precariously balanced against Kris's chest. "They've been lying around for a week, I bet. You always get a neatness fit when it's my day. Well, if you think I'm gonna do one of those dishes, you can just think again."

Kris glared at her. "You've got a real nerve, you know that? When you baked up your little package pizzas last night, the kitchen looked like — like a bomb went off in there. I never saw such a — "

Patsy posed, one fist where her waist might have been, had she narrowed at all around her lumpy middle. "I sure wish you'd make up your so-called mind exactly what you want," she said shrilly. "You go yelling to Mom because you never get any help with the cooking. But every time I bake — "

Kris picked it up, knowing it would be better to keep her mouth shut, well aware that Patsy deliberately baited her. "Any time you

13

bake," she said, "it's something to stuff in your own face. You ate half those pizzas before anybody even knew they were out of the oven."

She paused, vaguely aware that she had been missing something since she first came in the house. Of course. The dog hadn't come to meet her.

"Where's Jeb?"

Patsy shrugged and turned back to the mirror.

Puzzled, Kris took the dishes to the kitchen, then went to the back door. At her whistle, the old brown dog lying by the steps came to lick her hand, wagging the tail that looked like a piece of frayed rope, but without enthusiasm. His nose felt warm and dry, and it seemed to her that he walked slowly and carefully, as if it hurt him to move.

She sat down in the middle of the floor to put her arms around him, a cold hand squeezing her heart. "Jebber, are you sick?" she said softly. He had been listless the last few days. She had noticed that he hadn't been eating, that he slept a lot. But he was ten years old, and it had been hot the past week. She just hadn't thought too much about it.

Now, in a frantic attempt to make up for her neglect, she filled his water dish with fresh cool water. The dog drank a little, clearly trying to please. Then he lay down, head on paws, looking at her with dull sleepy eyes.

"Oh, Jeb," she said past the ache in her

throat. "You are sick, and nobody even noticed." She felt enormous guilt about that because everybody in the family considered him her dog.

Her father had brought him home as a fuzzy, endearingly awkward pup, all legs and eager pink tongue and busy tail. But as he grew, Kris was the one who fed him and gave him baths in a big tub in the backyard. She was the one who argued with her mother every time he was due for a rabies shot. Out of her baby-sitting money, she bought his flea collars and occasionally a rawhide bone, because her mother flatly refused to pay for "extras." He had trusted her more, loved her best. Now he was sick, and she hadn't even noticed.

"I'm sorry, boy. I've been so busy, but — we'll fix you up. I promise. You're all I have left, Jebber. When Mindy leaves, you'll be the only one."

She felt his nose again, scratched gently behind his ears and under his chin. Then she felt it, a lump on his throat. Again, something grabbed at her heart. A moment later, after dialing Mrs. Kelly's number, she talked over and through the cheerful burbling response.

"Oh, please, Mrs. Kelly, he's got to go to the vet right now. They're open till six. It wouldn't take long. Please!"

"All right, child, come get in the car. I'll just set my dinner back a little."

Kris hung up and went to tell Patsy, "I'll be

back in an hour, maybe sooner. If you want to eat before that, watch the vegetables. I was going to slice the rest of the pot roast and heat it with barbecue sauce, that bottle next to the mayonnaise."

Patsy shook her head. "We'll wait. I've got things to do. But you're really gonna catch it, you know. When Mom gets home — "

Kris ran back down the hall, not waiting to hear the rest. She knew her mother would be furious. All she ever thought about were the bills, what she considered necessary expenses. Everything else, she brushed aside as "things they could get along without."

Well, she could take the money out of that blasted college fund, Kris thought. Half of her baby-sitting earnings went into it. Her mother didn't have to act as if it weren't Kris's own money, or as if Jeb weren't a member of the family, too. He'd never cost them much, aside from having some bad teeth pulled. And hadn't her mother raised a storm over that bill!

She put Jeb in the back seat of Mrs. Kelly's old Plymouth and sat beside him, his head on her lap, catching only an occasional phrase of the neighbor's non-stop conversation on the way to the vet's.

"He'll be all right, honey," Mrs. Kelly said as they got out of the car. "These miracle drugs they got, why, they'll cure him right up. Don't you worry now."

But her round homely face looked anxious

as she watched the old dog walk into the office. Her eyes said she knew as well as Kris did that there was something seriously wrong.

The young veterinarian looked sober, too, once he had checked Jeb's heart and examined the swelling on his throat. He was kind enough to be honest.

"He's pretty well along in years. Heart's in good shape, though." He sighed. "We'll do some tests. But the way it looks at this point, chances are it's a tumor. If it's metastasized — I just don't know."

Kris held her breath for a moment. "Maybe — maybe surgery?"

He looked at her. "Can't say for sure right now," he said, his voice gentle. "We'll do the tests. You keep in touch."

Kris fought a fierce battle with the tears that threatened to spill over. She patted Jeb's head. "You stay, boy. Stay here. I'll be back to get you."

The dog's tail thumped feebly. He gave a soft whine as she walked to the door. When she looked back, he was lying with his head on his paws once more, watching her.

For once, Mrs. Kelly seemed to have run out of conversation. She made only a few distracted comments on the way home, meant to reassure, to comfort. But the tone of her voice acknowledged failure.

In the driveway, Kris paused before she opened the car door. "You're just about the best friend I've got," she said. "I always know I can count on you, Mrs. Kelly."

She was glad she had said it, though it embarrassed both of them. The woman's face turned bright pink, and her eyes filled with tears. She didn't say anything, just patted Kris's shoulder and went in her house. With the emotional Mrs. Kelly, a lump in her throat seemed to be the one thing that blocked the ceaseless flow of words.

Kris felt a little startled by the display of emotion from the twins, when she told them about Jeb at dinner. She hadn't expected much reaction. The old dog hadn't been playful for the past year or two. He slept a lot, though he followed Kris from room to room when she was home, curling himself in a corner to watch her, brown eyes adoring.

The twins had always considered him her dog, ignoring him for the most part. Still, the news about him seemed to hit them hard.

"You think he might — he might die?" Greg asked hoarsely. His dark eyes were wide, troubled.

"Jeb's as old as we are. That's awful old for a dog," Guy said, equally sober. "He could have a — a heart attack or something."

Patsy reached for the milk, watching Kris as she poured herself a second glass. She was supposed to limit herself on milk and butter and the pastry she spent all her money on. Kris could feel little sympathy for her sister's problems with her skin when she saw her eating constantly, always the worst things for her skin. *Lap it up*, Kris thought now. *If you break out with a dozen new lumps and bumps, it'll serve you right.*

As if she read her mind, Patsy gave her a faint unpleasant smile. "The one who's gonna have a heart attack around here will be Mom. Just wait till she finds out Jeb's at the vet's, staying overnight for a bunch of tests. Boy, is that gonna be one fantastic bill!"

Kris noted the sudden alarm on her brothers' faces and guessed what was going through their minds. They desperately wanted a bicycle for their birthday, two weeks away. The most they could hope for was one bicycle which they would share. At that, their mother had warned them bikes were so expensive, she would have to locate something secondhand, or they would be out of luck.

Now, without another word, they got up from the table and returned to their room, the bedroom door banging behind them.

Kris looked at Patsy. "Thanks," she said. "I'll remember that."

"I'm shaking with terror."

A few minutes later, Kris gave up the attempt at eating. She scraped the food from her plate in the dog's dish, then remembered where Jeb was.

Back in the room she shared with Patsy, she lay on her bed and stared at the ceiling as the room gradually darkened. Her thoughts rambled erratically, but it seemed as if everything added to her pain and anger, her fear about Jeb.

After a long time, Patsy opened the door to yell over the TV noise from the living room and the commotion from the twins' room across the hall. "It's after nine. Aren't you going to make them go to bed?"

"Why should I?"

"Because I can't even hear the TV." She glared at Kris, who neither moved nor spoke. "Boy, wait till Mom gets home — !"

When her mother opened the bedroom door at last, the boys had subsided, and their room was dark. The TV had been turned down, as well. Mrs. Wilding spoke in a low tone, however, as if she hadn't been told the whole story in detail, as if she actually thought the twins might be asleep.

"Come out in the kitchen. I want to talk to you."

Kris sighed, rolled off the bed and followed her mother down the hall, blinking in the light. She sat at the table, ignoring Patsy, who stood behind her mother at the sink, a wide grin on her face.

Mrs. Wilding turned abruptly. "Go to bed, Patsy."

"But I want to — "

"You want to listen while I give her hell.

I'm sure you do." Her mother made a sharp gesture. "Go to bed."

When she heard the bathroom door close, she straightened and looked at Kris. "Okay, suppose you start explaining a few things." Her voice was tight, barely hinting at the anger in her eyes.

"Since when have you been making the rules around here? Letting the twins run wild, imposing on Mrs. Kelly after all she does for us." She ended in a strained whisper. "Taking the dog and leaving him for a series of tests — ". She swallowed, her eyes very dark against the pallor of her skin.

"Just where do you think you get the right to make decisions like that?"

Kris saw the weariness on her face, dark smudges beneath her eyes. She noted all of it and hardened her heart, because in her mind, she saw a dog's pleading eyes, heard a soft whine.

"He's one of the family," she said in the stubborn tone with which she always argued his cause. "You can take the money out of the college fund."

Mrs. Wilding made a sudden movement that startled Kris so much, she almost dodged back. For a moment, she had thought her mother was going to slap her.

"The college fund!" The words emerged from between her teeth. "That isn't your money, and it isn't my money — not to pay any vet bills, it isn't. That money is for *college*."

She leaned against the drainboard, arms crossed, eyes burning in her small face. "Why can't you get it through your head, the most important thing in your life right now is getting ready for college. An education is your ticket to — to anything you want, any kind of life, any career. You can do a lot better than a job waiting on tables, earn really good money. Then you won't have to lean on some man, not if you don't want to. You can make it on your own, all by yourself."

Her head came forward, chin extended. "You're the one with the brains in the family. So why is it you can't understand something I've told you a hundred times? Why is it you don't even seem to care?"

Kris stared at her. "Why is it you don't care about a sick animal? How can you turn your back on Jeb after ten years?"

Mrs. Wilding made a short brushing movement with one hand. "Spare me the violins," she said in a tired voice. "Just hear me good now, and don't forget what I'm telling you. If you ever pull a stunt like that again, you'll be sorry, I promise you that."

Kris said nothing.

Her mother straightened her shoulders, but her gaze didn't waver. She said then, surprisingly, "You need to get out more. Too much studying isn't good, either."

Kris gave a brief laugh. "That isn't exactly my number one problem," she said. "You'd better brace yourself for my report card."

Her mother frowned. "No excuses for it," she said crossly. "You spend all your time with that trash down the street. Where you get your taste in friends is a real question. I saw her yesterday in a see-through blouse cut to the navel. No bra, either. She sure looked like a tramp."

Kris felt her temper rise in spite of her good intentions. "How would you know what Mindy's like? You're always at work or asleep when she comes over. If you are around, you sure don't make any secret about how you feel."

"Why don't you have any other friends?" her mother persisted.

"Because I'm always stuck at home, you know that. And the place is a mess, thanks to the twins and *their* friends. You think I want anybody but Mindy to see it the way it looks most of the time? And just how do you think I can get out more" — she underlined the words with sarcasm — "when you won't trust Patsy to baby-sit? She's fourteen. I'd been baby-sitting for years when I was her age."

She always felt sorry later when she opened up like that. All the stored-up grievances came out, but it never helped. It was as if they had knife-sharp edges that cut even as she got rid of them. And they always came back, making her increasingly angry until the next time she let fly.

Her mother turned away, waving the words aside. "That's enough," she said. "That's enough out of you. You aren't the only one around here with a problem."

Kris bit back a fiery retort. "What are you going to do — about Jeb?"

"I'll take care of it," her mother said. "Go on to bed. I've had enough for one day."

Join the club, Kris thought. She left the kitchen so quickly, she stumbled over Patsy crouched in the hall, listening. In a way, her sister was worse off than she was. At least, she had Mindy. Patsy had no friends at all.

Tonight, however, Kris could feel nothing toward her but resentment. She paused only long enough to say in a low bitter voice, "What a rotten little sneak you are."

Then she went in the bathroom and locked the door. Her nerves were strung so tight, she would have to take a warm shower to relax or she'd never get to sleep.

Chapter
Three

That night she dreamed about Jeb. Someone had stolen him, and she groped through drifting fog, hearing him whimper in the distance, knowing he was hurt or sick. When Mrs. Kelly appeared out of the darkness, Kris felt a vast relief. Mrs. Kelly would help.

But she was in a hurry. She paused only long enough to say, "Oh, they had to take your dog back to the vet's, you know. It was those miracle drugs, some kind of side-effect." And she bustled away.

It seemed in the dream as if she walked for hours trying to find the vet. Once she took a cab, then discovered that she had lost her money. She jumped out and ran, the angry driver chasing her. At last she found the place, a new office over a pizza parlor. She saw Patsy in a booth by the window, eating a family-size pizza all by herself.

But when she went upstairs and opened the door with the vet's name on it, she found the rooms deserted. The outer office looked the same as the one in their old quarters, and there were four examining rooms here, too. She opened the door of the first three to find them empty. But in the last, she found a dog's skeleton lying on the metal table, Jeb's green collar around the neck.

She woke sobbing, her pillow already damp with tears. For some reason, her grief persisted though she had come wide awake, her heart pounding, aware that it had been a nightmare. She cried for a long time.

The next morning, her eyes were swollen, and she had a dull headache most of the day. She couldn't get Jeb out of her mind, wishing she could go visit him, at least. Mrs. Kelly had told her that the tests would take a while, and it wouldn't do any good to call in the very next day.

Kris didn't want to ask the neighbor woman to take her there again. Visiting might not be permitted, anyway. Besides, Mrs. Kelly hadn't offered to take her back. All day, the feeling of horror and helplessness from the dream persisted, tormenting her each time she remembered how she had opened that fourth door and found the skeleton on the table.

It was even worse when she went home that afternoon, because there were reminders of Jeb all over the house, food dishes in the kitchen, his favorite pillow in the corner of the living room, the collar he had worn as a puppy on the mirror in her bedroom.

When the phone rang shortly after four, she ran to it, thinking it might be the vet's office. Jeb had been there for almost twenty-four hours. Possibly they had something to report.

But the voice on the line was young and male and vaguely familiar. She couldn't identify it. Struggling with a mixture of disappointment and relief, she told herself it had not been good news about Jeb, but neither had it been bad news.

"Kris? This is Regan."

She went completely blank for a moment even as she responded automatically, "Oh, hi, Regan."

In the space of a few seconds, her mind sorted through the file of sensory impressions for the face that matched the voice and the name. Oh, sure. Regan was the boy who sat behind her in English, a kind of average-looking boy, except for a great smile.

Shy. He didn't talk much, except about homework assignments, though he always smiled when they met in the halls. Regan was his last name, actually. He had a ridiculous first name, O'Flaherity or O'Shaugnessey, something of the sort. So everybody called him Regan.

"Hi," he said again. "I wasn't sure you'd remember."

"Yes. Second period English," she said and thought how stupid she sounded. A boy hadn't called her for a long time. It wasn't as if she'd ever had a whole lot of experience, talking to boys.

"The reason I'm calling," he said and paused for several seconds. "I wondered if you'd like to — well, there's a good flick on at the drive-in. If you like Robert Redford — "

Kris laughed, her own awkwardness vanishing as she pictured the poor guy, probably turning red because he was so shy, but smiling.

"I don't know anybody who doesn't like Robert Redford."

"Great. Hey, would you like to go then? Friday night?"

She almost said no. There were so many problems, it never seemed worth the hassle, not for the few boys who had shown interest in her up till now.

Somehow, Regan was different. Not that he was a boy she'd dream about, the kind who made her stomach go hollow when she thought about them, but he was nice. She would feel comfortable with him. She could talk to him without getting her words twisted up so everything came out sounding so dumb.

"Yes, I'd like to go," she said and thought, why not? Her mother had told her last night she needed to get out more. Let her figure some way to manage it.

"Great! I'll pick you up about 7:30, okay?"

Kris hung up, wondering what she should wear. The pink blouse, perhaps, and the denims she saved for special days. Mindy said pink looked good on her. She felt a twinge of excitement, thinking about Friday and Regan and a real date. The movie was supposed to be terrific, too.

As she headed for the bedroom to check the outfit she had planned in her mind, she heard the bathroom door close softly. Then, in the hall, she stopped short as she caught a whiff of her mother's lilac perfume.

Patsy! She had been into her mother's things again. And she had been listening to the conversation with Regan. Kris stood watching the door, anger rising inside.

From the backyard, the boys' voices came clearly through the kitchen window.

"It's my turn."

"You had it last time."

"I did not!"

"Did, too!"

Still Kris waited, leaning against the wall. At

last the bathroom door opened and Patsy came out, humming to herself. She stopped, startled, when she saw her sister.

"What're you doing? What's the matter?"

Kris said evenly, "There's a name for people like you, people who listen at keyholes and paw through things that don't belong to them and help themselves. There's a nasty ugly name. In fact, I can think of several. Every time you take a piece of paper and write Patsy Elaine Wilding, you can add one of them in parentheses."

Her voice rose as she listed them, slowly, emphatically. "Snoop. Sneak. Thief. Take your pick."

Patsy's head jerked back. As she flushed, the blemishes on her face stood out clearly. She mimicked Kris's words, her voice mocking. "*I don't know anybody who doesn't like Robert Redford.*"

"Creep," Kris muttered and went by her into the bedroom.

"How you think you're gonna get out Friday night, anyway? That's Mom's late night. You plan to take the twins with you?" Patsy laughed. "If you think I'll watch them, you got another think coming."

Kris picked up her sister's shoes, over on her side of the room, as usual. Whirling, she threw them at the grinning face in the doorway.

Patsy dodged, and the shoes hit the wall behind her, leaving black marks on the faded pink wallpaper. She laughed as she ran to the kitchen. "Fat chance you got for your big romantic date! Just you wait till Mom hears."

Kris slammed the door and threw herself across the bed, shaking with frustration and anger. She had forgotten that Friday was her mother's night for the late shift. But it probably wouldn't make any difference what night had been chosen. Patsy had been right about that. Fat chance, indeed, for a date, for any kind of fun, when there was neither money nor opportunity to get out as other girls did.

She didn't cry. She had used up all her tears last night. After a long time, her anger drained away. She was simply too tired to hold onto it, her eyes too heavy to stay open staring at the wall.

She slept so hard, the twins had to shake her awake.

"Hey, how about dinner? We're hungry! There isn't anything even started yet. And Patsy ate up all the cookies that were supposed to go in lunches. There isn't enough milk to go around, either. She drank all but just a little bit, the pig! Wake up, willya?"

Kris blinked at their cross faces. "What time is it?"

"Almost seven. And we're hungry!"

She sat up slowly, more drugged than refreshed from her sleep. Even when she washed her face with cold water, she couldn't seem to shake off the dull lethargic feeling. She went out to warm meatloaf from the night before, fixed some rice to go with it, and opened a can of corn, her hands moving automatically without much help from her brain.

The twins were pleased with the cocoa she made from canned milk, so there would be enough fresh milk for cereal the next morning. She found herself thinking, why did it matter? Why should she worry about it? Was it her responsibility?

It had been for a long time, and even in her present uncaring mood she went on planning and working things out as if it really were important, just as she always did.

After dinner, she did the dishes, then washed the tee shirt she wanted to wear tomorrow and some of her underwear. When their washing machine finally broke down a few months ago, her mother decided it would be cheaper to use the laundromat nearby. But Kris found the heat in the driers too high for delicate fabrics, even at the lowest setting. She preferred washing her own things by hand to keep them looking nice as long as possible.

She didn't go to check the pink blouse. There would be time for that tomorrow. She felt a faint, almost superstitious, reluctance about doing anything positive, about making any kind of plans for that date. Maybe she would be going out Friday night, she thought wearily, and maybe she wouldn't.

Again, she felt the hateful constrictions on

her life as if they were tangible bonds that kept her tied in the same unpleasant rut, performing on schedule like a robot.

She might feel different about it if anyone said thank-you, expressed appreciation in any way, but no one ever did. The twins begged for a pie or cake once in a while, then told her what a great cook she was, and that was about it. Her mother was too bitter about being overworked and tired all the time, herself, to notice the load anybody else carried, let alone comment about it.

Kris went to hang her laundry on the shower-curtain rod, knowing no one would take a bath until she insisted on it. She wouldn't. Tonight, she wouldn't care if the roof fell in around them.

As she straightened, she glanced at her reflection in the mirrored door of the medicine cabinet. How much she looked like her mother, she thought, appalled. Because it was more than a strong physical resemblance. In that moment, she saw an identical expression, a slight frown, a tightness pulling her mouth into a hard line.

The sudden unwary glimpse left her badly shaken. What will become of me? she wondered, chilled by the sight of that stranger in the mirror, the girl who looked so much older than she, so tired and unhappy.

Would she turn into a worn, bitter woman like her mother, nagging and yelling at kids of her own? Was that why her father had taken off, because he couldn't stand any more, because he couldn't please her mother, either?

She pushed the thoughts aside and went quickly to get her books and settle at the kitchen table. A book report was long overdue, and she hoped the teacher wouldn't mark her down because of that. She had not read the book, a biography of Amelia Earhart, though it looked interesting. There seemed to be so little time lately for reading or studying. Besides, Patsy always had the TV on full blast, and the boys made so much noise in their bedroom it made it hard to concentrate.

Twice this semester, she had chosen biographies for the assigned book reports. If she actually found time, she enjoyed reading about someone's fascinating life. And if she didn't get around to finishing the book, it was easier to fake a report when most of the details were spelled out on the dust cover.

She was just completing the assignment when her mother came in the front door. Patsy must have bounced up to greet her, because their voices murmured on and on for several minutes before the TV went off. When her sister went down the hall, Kris did not look up. She sat with her head propped on one hand, waiting. At last her mother came out to heat some water for coffee.

Mrs. Wilding didn't speak immediately,

reaching for a mug and the jar of instant coffee, rummaging in the drawer for a spoon.

Unable to stand the silence any longer, Kris took a deep breath and asked, "Well, did you get your daily report?"

It surprised her a little when her mother turned to say sharply, "You've sure developed a mean tongue lately. I want you to watch it. Always complaining about the kids giving you a hard time — well, maybe you'd get along a whole lot better if you didn't jump at every last thing they do."

Kris stared, her mouth open until she became aware of it and snapped it shut. Of all people to talk about a mean tongue! She waited a few minutes, trying to cool off, but it didn't help. A fiery ball of anger in her chest grew with every passing second.

It was difficult to speak past it. "All right," she said, "how about Friday night? I mean, you said you thought I should get out."

"Oh, come off it," her mother said impatiently. She didn't bother to pretend she hadn't been briefed about Kris's date. "You don't have to take that self-righteous tone, either, or feel so damned sorry for yourself. Sometimes I think you deliberately make plans like this. Then when someone tells you they're impossible, you can act the poor abused orphan. You know Friday's my late night, and you go right ahead and make plans for Friday."

"Suppose I change the night?" Kris felt her face flush, but she forced a small mocking smile. "Would it really make a difference?"

Her mother opened her mouth, then turned away to grasp the handle of the tea kettle and stand for a moment, staring down at it.

"I don't get home until 9:30," she said. "If Patsy would take over for an hour or two, you might try to work it out sometime, I suppose. But she certainly doesn't sound in any mood tonight to do you any favors."

A short silence.

"I might have known," Kris said. "You're going to push it all off on me. If I can't work out something with Patsy, it's *my* fault, because I haven't been nice to her, because I can't get along with her. Is that it?"

"Spare me," her mother said shortly. She made a sweeping gesture with one hand. "Kris, I don't want to argue about it."

Kris got to her feet, swallowing hard, anger churning in her stomach, an ominous bitterness at the back of her throat.

"One more thing," her mother said as she reached the door.

Kris turned and thought, for a fleeting moment, her mother looked ill. She seemed paler than usual, a drawn expression around her mouth. But when she lifted the mug to drink, her face seemed entirely normal again.

"I called about the dog."

Kris stiffened. "What — what did they say?"

Mrs. Wilding sighed. "They said just about what I expected them to say. Jeb had a tumor. We can't afford surgery, and we most certainly can't pay for a lot of expensive tests, either, to find out whether it — "

She paused, then went on quickly. "He was ten years old. It wouldn't have been right to let him — to let him go on the way he was. Already it was bothering him. That's why you noticed — something was wrong."

She turned away from Kris's burning gaze. "It's a fact of *life* around here," she said with an odd emphasis on the word. "We don't have much money. And what we do have has to go for essential things." She went through the familar litany as if she hadn't said it fifty times before with varying emotion, everything from irritation to weary resignation.

Kris said into the silence, spacing the words with care, afraid she might lose her dinner right there on the kitchen floor, *"What did you tell them?"*

"I had him put to sleep."

Patsy was just emerging from the bathroom when Kris brushed her aside roughly, slamming the door between them. She stayed on her knees in front of the john long after the spasms had stopped and her breathing returned to normal. She sat with her eyes closed, scrubbing at her mouth with a wad of tissue. Silently, fiercely, she told herself, *Mindy was right, Mindy was right.*

And because that seemed to help shut out the other images, the other thoughts that threatened to flood over her, hurting more than she could stand to be hurt, she began to whisper the words over and over.

"Mindy was right. Mindy was right. I've got to get away from here!"

Chapter
Four

When she saw Regan in English the next day, she told him that her mother had restricted her, so she wouldn't be able to go out Friday night. It seemed the simplest way to handle the situation, and what she said was true enough, merely lacking a few details.

Regan nodded, looking resigned. "Happens," he said. "When do you get your parole?"

"Well, that's a question." Kris shook her head. "Only five more days of school and — I don't think I'll be around very long after that."

"Going somewhere on vacation?"

"Uh, yes, in a way." She saw him studying her with a slight smile. On impulse, she told him, "I don't think I'll be back. Things at home are — I just can't take it anymore."

His smile vanished. Just as the bell rang, he leaned forward to say under the rustling of papers and the last minute burst of conversation around them, "Kris, don't do anything crazy. You aren't planning to hitch a ride wherever you're going?"

"Oh, no. I won't be alone."

"Good." His eyes flickered to the next aisle where Mindy sat with her head on her folded arms on the desk. "Matter of fact, I'll be leaving right after school's out, too. I'm spending the summer with my uncle and aunt down in San Diego." He looked at her with his quick bright smile. "Any chance you're heading in that direction?"

Kris hesitated. Actually, Mindy and Clip would be going to the San Diego area. But for good reason, none of them would be looking up any friends down there.

"I'm not sure where I'll be," she said in a half truth. "I'm sorry about the movie, Regan."

Again he nodded, adding something about a raincheck.

Kris turned away as the teacher spoke to Mindy, and she straightened in her seat, looking sleepy and bored.

That morning on the way to school, Kris had told her that she had made up her mind to leave. At first, Mindy didn't seem to take her seriously. The way she acted, it was almost as if she regretted extending the invitation to go along.

"You sure about this?" She hugged her notebook to her chest, peering down at her feet in the ragged tennies. Finally she glanced at Kris. "It's no picnic on the road, you know. That old van of Clip's, it don't offer much in the way of luxury."

Kris said evenly, "If you'd rather I made other arrangements — "

"No, no, don't get me wrong. Of course I want you along. It's just that you have to understand how it'll be."

"Don't worry, I have a pretty good idea."

"Okay." Mindy sighed, her steps slowing as she went on, sounding awkward now, almost embarrassed.

"Do you think — could you get some money, somehow? I mean, well, I'd be glad to pay your way if I could, but — " She made a wry face. "We'll need money for food, for gas. You know."

"Sure."

Clip would insist that she pay her share, Kris thought. He'd probably think she should pay more than that, seeing what a great favor he was doing, letting her ride along. She could only guess, of course, at the way his mind worked behind those narrow black eyes that saw so much and liked so little of what they saw.

"How much do you think would be fair?" she asked, her voice tentative.

"Fifty dollars?" Mindy added hastily, "I've got a phony I.D., you know, and I look older. I can always get a job slingin' hash. I've done it before. But you look so young, it isn't as if you could — well, you won't be able to contribute much later on. And that could be a problem." Her voice trailed, delicately avoiding spelling out the difficulty.

Kris was silent for a moment as they joined the stragglers hurrying for their first class. *Fifty dollars*, she thought, aghast.

"How would I manage then?" she asked. "I mean, when that money's gone?"

Mindy made an airy gesture, one plump hand describing an arc, palm up. "We're going to a place just this side of the border for a couple weeks, a kind of commune. Then we'll head for Arizona. And you're a real good cook. I mean, you could probably work something out easy, once we get there."

With growing enthusiasm, she began to plan for the journey. "I can lend you a zipper bag my old man left behind. You'll have to take everything you got that's really nice. Your pink blouse, all your good stuff. I mean, why leave anything for old Patsy to glom onto?"

Kris nodded uncertainly.

"You think you can get the money?"

The last of June, Kris thought. Her mother would cash that check to pay the rent and the utility bills. Yes, she could get the money and leave a note, telling her mother to take it out of the college fund. She had earned at least that much. It wasn't as if she'd be taking anything that wasn't hers.

What chance did she have to go to college, anyway? At least, this way she could get by until she could make it on her own, some place away from people who pulled at her and pushed at her and yelled at her all the time. Anything would be an improvement over life at present with a cold unloving mother who ordered a dog killed just because he didn't have a high enough priority.

She blinked hard, the books on her locker shelf blurring for a moment as she reached for them.

"Yes," she told Mindy, her voice quiet, "I can get the money."

As if she read her mind, Mindy echoed her thoughts. "You must have given your mom at least fifty dollars for that college fund she's always yakking about."

She laughed. "And if she hasn't really been putting your money away like she says she has, well, it'll be a good joke on her."

She saw Kris's face tighten and went on, softly, "Anybody who'd do what she did to a really great dog — " She shook her head.

Kris didn't want to talk about it. She couldn't bear even to think about it anymore. If only time would go by quickly, she thought. She couldn't wait to leave and begin a new life somewhere far away.

Somehow, the days passed, full of her usual activities at home. The zipper bag hidden under her bed gradually filled with clean mended clothes and mementos that had special meaning for her: Jeb's collar; a Hummel figurine she had won in an eighth grade essay contest; a charm bracelet Mrs. Kelly had given her.

Last winter, Mrs. Kelly had been ill, and Kris took care of her all during Christmas vacation. It hadn't interfered with any plans. It wasn't as if she had given up a lot of parties or dates. In fact, she found it quite restful in Mrs. Kelly's quiet kitchen making jello and soup and pudding, in contrast with the bedlam at home. She felt a little guilty about the bracelet. It came from a good store, and she knew Mrs. Kelly couldn't afford gifts like that.

"No, not another word," the woman said when Kris protested. "I only wish I could do more. After all your help, honey, that's little enough in the way of a thank you."

On the last night, Kris tucked a bath towel on top of her clothes and zipped the bag shut. There wasn't room for anything else. She decided to put the extra things into a tote bag her mother had discarded when one of the woven handles broke. Soap, a wash cloth, toothbrush and paste went into that. She might need them before she reached San Diego, anyway.

It was close to midnight when she got out of bed and dressed quietly, pausing occasionally to listen to Patsy's even breathing in the next bed. Her sister lay on her side, facing the window, hair spread across the pillow, her round face relaxed and vulnerable in sleep.

Kris wondered if she would ever see Patsy and the boys again. Then, a cold, lost feeling flooding over her, she straightened her shoulders and deliberately recaptured a few of her more unpleasant memories.

Of course she would see them again, she thought. A good long separation wouldn't be a bad thing for any of them. Patsy had a lot to learn about getting along with people, growing out of her preoccupation with herself. With her big sister gone, there would be pressure on her to shape up, and that might be the best thing that ever happened to her.

She wouldn't be able to sleep in the mornings until the last minute. She'd have to get up and make breakfast. With a sudden sharp twinge, Kris thought, *would Patsy do that?* But she couldn't stop to worry about it. She was already behind schedule.

Fumbling in her pocket for the note she had written that afternoon, she put it on her pillow. The note had been a difficult one to write. She discarded a half dozen versions before she decided to make it short and simple and unemotional.

Her mother would know very well why she

was running away. It wasn't necessary to give any reasons, to justify the action, and it was too late for accusations.

"Mother," she wrote at last, feeling only numbness inside, welcoming the emptiness after the turmoil of anger and hurt. "I am going away. Please don't try to find me and bring me back. I would only leave again, the first chance I got. I am taking fifty dollars from your purse. You can get it out of the college fund."

She read it through quickly, added three words in the last line, "of my money," and signed her name.

Now, quietly, she felt her way down the hall, edging along the wall to avoid the squeaky boards in the middle. As the front door closed behind her with a soft final click, she went down the steps, hurried across the lawn, and broke into a run as she reached the street.

She could see Clip's van parked in Mindy's drive, and she heard someone laugh when she was still half a block away. Mindy's mother must be out of it again, Kris thought. They weren't even bothering to be quiet as they loaded the van.

Clip straightened as she approached and stood, fists on narrow hips, staring at her. In the dim light, she could see a crooked smile, almost a grimace, twisting his thin lips.

"Did you get all the kiddies tucked in?" he inquired in the rough, gritty voice she detested.

"I guess you know you held us up a good three hours. We coulda been there by now."

Kris said nothing as she reached past him to put her bag in the back of the van. He slammed the door and went to get behind the wheel. A moment later, Mindy ran down the walk.

"Hi," she said to Kris, her voice breathless, excited. "Have any trouble getting out?" She slid in beside Clip and Kris joined her, swinging the door shut.

Over the sound of the engine, she said, "No problem."

Mindy grinned. "No second thoughts? I figured you might back out at the last minute."

Kris shook her head. "Why would I do that? If I don't know what I'm getting into, well, I sure know what I'm leaving behind."

For a while, she felt keyed up with nerves and a certain apprehension. The van had covered several miles by the time she stopped looking in the side mirror for some sign of pursuit, though she couldn't have said what she thought that might be.

A police car, perhaps, checking suspicious looking vehicles for runaways. An hour later on the freeway going south, she began to wind down, struggling to stay awake, unhappily aware that the sullen, silent Clip was angry because she had come along.

Just outside Oceanside, he went down a ramp and pulled into an all-night hamburger place.

"Gotta get some coffee," he said. The note of anger was still in his voice. "I'm beat. If we coulda got away sooner — "

"Oh, hush." Mindy slid across the seat on his side and stood whispering to him fiercely for several moments before they followed Kris into the restaurant.

When they had given their orders to the gaunt puffy-eyed waitress on duty, Clip looked across the table at Kris. "Let's have the bread," he said, extending a hand with square dirty nails.

She stared at him, too tired to understand what he meant or even to care.

Mindy intervened. "He means the money you brought," she said and slapped his hand aside. But she gave him a quick smile to show she was teasing. "Look, I'm not going to stand in the middle anymore. If you two want to slug it out toe-to-toe, great. Just leave me out of it."

Kris said carefully, "I want to pay my way, sure. But why should I give you all my money right at the start?"

"You want a good reason?" He leaned forward, his voice rough. "Because I'm gonna leave you here if you don't. It's up to you, Baby Girl."

Their food arrived, creating a small diversion. When Clip went to the counter for the catsup, Mindy said in an urgent whisper, "Give me the money, Kris. It'll be all right when he sees I got it. Later on, I can slip it back to you, okay? Don't worry. He's just in a mood to-night."

Kris hesitated, uneasily aware that she had no choice. If only she could be sure that Mindy would handle the situation later on. Handing the money over, she turned to her food. The hamburger was tough and tasteless, but she ate hungrily. She hadn't been able to eat much dinner, her stomach jumping with nerves as she watched the clock mark off her last hours at home.

Clip seemed to thaw with each cup of the strong black coffee. He inquired at last with his mocking crooked smile, "What you gonna do, Baby Girl, when all your money's used up?"

"I don't know," she said, trying to sound casual about it. "Mindy said I could work something out when we get there. I'm a good cook."

His smile sagged, then widened as he erupted with harsh, strident laughter. "So she said you could work something out," he said and shook his head, still chuckling. "I wouldn't be a bit surprised, at that. Some of those old boys might like your style, who knows? If they got a taste for young stuff — "

"Oh, knock it off!" Mindy told him crossly. "Think you're so funny." She got to her feet and jerked her head toward the restroom door. "Come on," she said to Kris. "Let the come-dian simmer down while we make a visit."

Minutes later, the van swung onto the freeway. Mindy's head began to nod, coming to rest eventually on Kris's shoulder. But sleep eluded Kris. She stared at the scattered lights of oncoming traffic, Clip's amused voice in her mind.

A taste for young stuff . . . Cold fear lay in her stomach like a heavy block of ice. What had he meant by that? What was she getting into?

They had just passed the first few ramps into Chula Vista when she heard Clip swearing softly.

He glanced at her. "Black-and-white pacing us." His scowl said this, too, was her fault. "We better pull off the road."

"Where?"

"Anywhere! Watch for a side road, dummy, *any* road."

"There!" she said. "Just ahead. But it's an open field — "

He turned, anyway, onto a rutted dirt road. The headlights picked out a packing shed a short distance in, and he parked on the far side.

Mindy sat up, instantly alert, sensing something wrong the moment her eyes opened. "What's the matter?"

Clip flicked off the lights and cut the motor. "Cop pacing us." He grunted, peering toward the freeway. "It's okay. He didn't stop." He leaned back, rubbing his eyes.

"Can we go on?"

ours since Mindy had told her they
for food.

ng to her feet, stiff from her hard,
she went to look out the door. The
ne, yet the sun's position told her it
e or ten o'clock by now. What could
ned to Mindy and Clip?

d away, her heart beating rapidly,
sensation in her throat from the
cted rhythm. Then she stopped to
place where she had left her zipper

ll her clothes, everything but the
she had packed in the tote bag —
hat why Mindy had come into the
down at her with that odd intent
face?

it hadn't been her fault. Clip must
her into leaving on the pretext of
He hadn't wanted Kris along. He
ade any secret of the way he felt
ssenger he called Baby Girl, biting
s abrasive voice.

nent, her mind swerved back and
fact and the fiction she tried to
No, she told herself at last, she
the truth. At this point, she had
enormity of her predicament so
omething about it.

she knew for a fact that Mindy
Clip in his worst moods when she
e often boasted about it. No one

"Maybe it wouldn't be too smart. If we ran
into him up ahead — that's all we'd need, a
lot of questions at two in the morning."

Mindy sighed, resigned, flexible under any
conditions. "Okay, let's get some sleep and go
on when it's light." She leaned forward, looking past Clip's shoulder. "What's that?"

"Packing shed." He got out of the van and
disappeared into the shadows for a moment.
There was a sharp metallic snap, followed by
the sound of creaky hinges.

He reappeared at the window to announce,
"Open for occupancy. You want to bed down
by yourself, Baby Girl?"

"Oh. Okay, sure." Kris stirred, released from
the spell of a nightmare that was all too real.
Her right foot had gone to sleep. She stumbled
on her way to the back of the van to get the
zipper bag.

"What do you want with that?" Mindy said
at her shoulder.

"I can use the bath towel for a pillow." She
went through the door of the shed warily, pausing until her eyes became accustomed to the
dim light from a small, dirty window.

The place smelled of rotten wood from the
packing crates stacked along the walls, of damp
earth and decaying vegetables. It took several
minutes before she could bring herself to stretch
out on the hard dirt floor, her head on the tote
bag padded by the towel.

She lay for a long time, cold and uncomfortable, keenly aware of the slightest sound. There might be rats around a place where there were scraps of food. Her mind scurried after every fragmentary thought, quivering as it registered each sound, like a small scared animal. She forced herself back from the edge of panic, breathing slowly and deeply, clinging to the faint reassurance of plans for tomorrow.

She would have to go on her own as soon as possible, she thought, get away from Clip. She would size up the situation and the people when they reached their destination. Maybe one of the girls could help. At least she'd know more about her options than she did right now. There was no sense in staying awake worrying about what lay ahead. She needed to rest. She was terribly tired.

Just as she drifted off to sleep, she thought, absurdly, she had forgotten to cut the twins' hair. It was a job she put off as long as possible because they gave her such a hard time, jerking and wiggling and yelling at her for taking too much off. She had gone away, forgetting all about it, and they needed a haircut so badly.

Chapt
Five

She woke
shack. Still g
standing ove
fixed express
"Is it tim
"No. Sorr
you a note.
on the way.
sleep, okay?
Some tin
freeway br
noticing u
had chang
of dirt on

couple of h
were going
Scrambl
lumpy bed,
van was go
must be nin
have happe
She turn
a choking
pulsing refl
stare at the
bag.
Gone! A
few articles
gone. Was t
shed to star
look on her
Oh, surely
have bullied
getting food.
had never m
about the pa
sarcasm in h
For a mon
forth betwee
force upon it
had to accep
to know the
she could do
Well, then,
could handle
wanted to. Sh

52

had forced her to go into the packing shed and take the zipper bag. Mindy had lied about her errand as easily and skillfully as Kris had seen her lie to others.

Her mother had been right about Mindy, after all, she thought, and found the admission even more painful because of the hurt of betrayal. Okay, it didn't change the fact that her mother was wrong about everything else. It didn't mean she would go home even if that were possible. She had merely been used by one more person, someone she considered a friend, somebody she had trusted. She resolved fiercely not to make that mistake again.

At the sound of an engine, she turned back to the window, heart pounding once more. An old pickup truck bumped its way past, several Mexicans riding in back. They must be workers on their way to the other end of the field, Kris thought, and knew she had to get out of the shed. Someone might discover her at any moment.

Rolling up her towel, she stuffed it into the tote bag. Outside, she checked the padlock that Clip had broken open last night, replacing it to look as before. Then, fighting the urge to run, she made herself walk slowly up the road.

As she headed for the closest ramp, she thought wryly she should just act as if she were out for a casual stroll, as if people made a habit of getting their exercise by walking on the shoulder of a freeway.

The people in the cars that whizzed past probably could guess what she was with one glance, she thought. She might as well wear a sign on her back in big block letters. *Runaway*.

Though it felt like the longest walk of her life, it must have been less than half a mile to the ramp and the street beyond that led into the business district. Kris felt limp with relief, released from the prolonged strain, when she finally reached the sidewalk.

Spotting a gas station nearby, she turned toward it. In the restroom, she waited for two ladies ahead of her who were chattering happily about the shopping they planned to do. Kris locked the outer door behind them. Then, quickly, she washed her face and hands, brushed her teeth and combed her hair. As she repacked her toilet articles, she was grateful for the impulse that had made her tuck them in a plastic bag.

Back on the sidewalk, she paused briefly at a small building nearby, noting the sign: Visitor's Bureau, Tourist Information. When she went on down the street, there was a map of Chula Vista in her bag and a brochure outlining points of interest.

During the next hour or so, she wandered through the business district, marking the location of public buildings such as the library and postoffice on her map, the grocery stores, Sears, and a large department store.

Finally, so hungry her stomach hurt, she

"Maybe it wouldn't be too smart. If we ran into him up ahead — that's all we'd need, a lot of questions at two in the morning."

Mindy sighed, resigned, flexible under any conditions. "Okay, let's get some sleep and go on when it's light." She leaned forward, looking past Clip's shoulder. "What's that?"

"Packing shed." He got out of the van and disappeared into the shadows for a moment. There was a sharp metallic snap, followed by the sound of creaky hinges.

He reappeared at the window to announce, "Open for occupancy. You want to bed down by yourself, Baby Girl?"

"Oh. Okay, sure." Kris stirred, released from the spell of a nightmare that was all too real. Her right foot had gone to sleep. She stumbled on her way to the back of the van to get the zipper bag.

"What do you want with that?" Mindy said at her shoulder.

"I can use the bath towel for a pillow." She went through the door of the shed warily, pausing until her eyes became accustomed to the dim light from a small, dirty window.

The place smelled of rotten wood from the packing crates stacked along the walls, of damp earth and decaying vegetables. It took several minutes before she could bring herself to stretch out on the hard dirt floor, her head on the tote bag padded by the towel.

She lay for a long time, cold and uncomfortable, keenly aware of the slightest sound. There might be rats around a place where there were scraps of food. Her mind scurried after every fragmentary thought, quivering as it registered each sound, like a small scared animal. She forced herself back from the edge of panic, breathing slowly and deeply, clinging to the faint reassurance of plans for tomorrow.

She would have to go on her own as soon as possible, she thought, get away from Clip. She would size up the situation and the people when they reached their destination. Maybe one of the girls could help. At least she'd know more about her options than she did right now. There was no sense in staying awake worrying about what lay ahead. She needed to rest. She was terribly tired.

Just as she drifted off to sleep, she thought, absurdly, she had forgotten to cut the twins' hair. It was a job she put off as long as possible because they gave her such a hard time, jerking and wiggling and yelling at her for taking too much off. She had gone away, forgetting all about it, and they needed a haircut so badly.

Chapter
Five

She woke to find a gray light filling the little shack. Still groggy with sleep, she saw Mindy standing over her, looking at her with an odd fixed expression.

"Is it time to go?" Kris mumbled.

"No. Sorry I woke you. I was going to leave you a note. We want to go get some food to eat on the way. Be right back. You get some more sleep, okay?"

Some time later, the rumble of traffic on the freeway brought Kris fully awake. She sat up, noticing uneasily that the quality of the light had changed. Sunlight sifted through the crust of dirt on the window. She must have slept a couple of hours since Mindy had told her they were going for food.

Scrambling to her feet, stiff from her hard, lumpy bed, she went to look out the door. The van was gone, yet the sun's position told her it must be nine or ten o'clock by now. What could have happened to Mindy and Clip?

She turned away, her heart beating rapidly, a choking sensation in her throat from the pulsing reflected rhythm. Then she stopped to stare at the place where she had left her zipper bag.

Gone! All her clothes, everything but the few articles she had packed in the tote bag — gone. Was that why Mindy had come into the shed to stare down at her with that odd intent look on her face?

Oh, surely it hadn't been her fault. Clip must have bullied her into leaving on the pretext of getting food. He hadn't wanted Kris along. He had never made any secret of the way he felt about the passenger he called Baby Girl, biting sarcasm in his abrasive voice.

For a moment, her mind swerved back and forth between fact and the fiction she tried to force upon it. No, she told herself at last, she had to accept the truth. At this point, she had to know the enormity of her predicament so she could do something about it.

Well, then, she knew for a fact that Mindy could handle Clip in his worst moods when she wanted to. She often boasted about it. No one

had forced her to go into the packing shed and take the zipper bag. Mindy had lied about her errand as easily and skillfully as Kris had seen her lie to others.

Her mother had been right about Mindy, after all, she thought, and found the admission even more painful because of the hurt of betrayal. Okay, it didn't change the fact that her mother was wrong about everything else. It didn't mean she would go home even if that were possible. She had merely been used by one more person, someone she considered a friend, somebody she had trusted. She resolved fiercely not to make that mistake again.

At the sound of an engine, she turned back to the window, heart pounding once more. An old pickup truck bumped its way past, several Mexicans riding in back. They must be workers on their way to the other end of the field, Kris thought, and knew she had to get out of the shed. Someone might discover her at any moment.

Rolling up her towel, she stuffed it into the tote bag. Outside, she checked the padlock that Clip had broken open last night, replacing it to look as before. Then, fighting the urge to run, she made herself walk slowly up the road.

As she headed for the closest ramp, she thought wryly she should just act as if she were out for a casual stroll, as if people made a habit of getting their exercise by walking on the shoulder of a freeway.

The people in the cars that whizzed past probably could guess what she was with one glance, she thought. She might as well wear a sign on her back in big block letters. *Runaway*.

Though it felt like the longest walk of her life, it must have been less than half a mile to the ramp and the street beyond that led into the business district. Kris felt limp with relief, released from the prolonged strain, when she finally reached the sidewalk.

Spotting a gas station nearby, she turned toward it. In the restroom, she waited for two ladies ahead of her who were chattering happily about the shopping they planned to do. Kris locked the outer door behind them. Then, quickly, she washed her face and hands, brushed her teeth and combed her hair. As she repacked her toilet articles, she was grateful for the impulse that had made her tuck them in a plastic bag.

Back on the sidewalk, she paused briefly at a small building nearby, noting the sign: Visitor's Bureau, Tourist Information. When she went on down the street, there was a map of Chula Vista in her bag and a brochure outlining points of interest.

During the next hour or so, she wandered through the business district, marking the location of public buildings such as the library and postoffice on her map, the grocery stores, Sears, and a large department store.

Finally, so hungry her stomach hurt, she

bought a loaf of day-old bread, a package of sliced cheese, and three oranges. She was tempted to get milk, too, but decided at last she simply couldn't afford it.

For now, she must buy the cheapest, most filling food, things she could carry easily that would last until she could earn some money. In this heat, she would have to consider, too, that things like milk and meat spoiled quickly. She couldn't risk getting sick.

In a small park close to the shopping area, she ate a sandwich and one of the oranges. Afterwards, in the restroom, she drank thirstily from her cupped hands, though the water in the faucet was lukewarm and it smelled faintly of chlorine. She went back to stretch out on the warm grass. It was time to make some plans.

She had exactly ninety-six cents left in her wallet. As she lifted her head after counting it, she saw three boys coming down the path nearby, looking at her. On impulse, she tucked the coins into a handkerchief in the pocket of her sweater before she replaced the wallet. The boys reminded her of Clip with their grimy clothes, greasy hair, and the kind of hard eyes that looked for the dirt in the world around them. From now on, Kris thought, she would trust no one. She had to assume that everyone she met was out to rip her off in some way. For a while, that was how it had to be.

At home, they would have found her note

by now, and things would be in more of an uproar than usual. Her mother might even be mad enough to cry, Kris mused.

Aside from yelling all the time, that seemed the only way her mother let off steam. When she was really angry, tears would stream down her thin, contorted face, making it hard for her to talk, let alone raise her voice. Still, those were the times all the kids jumped to obey or scurried off to hide. Her tears were the signal that she was in a red-hot rage about something.

Think about it another time, Kris told herself, drowsy from the warmth of the sun on her head, but afraid to nap. Somebody might take her food or run off with the old tote bag. Besides, she had to plan what to do. The most important thing right now was to find a place to sleep. Luckily, the weather was warm. She wouldn't get too cold at night, even if she slept outdoors.

She looked around at the little park, considering it for a moment. This grassy slope felt a lot softer than her bed on the hard dirt floor of the shed last night. Then she heard a burst of hoarse laughter from the other side of the restrooms, and she decided reluctantly that the park wouldn't be a safe place after dark. Where then?

When someone behind her spoke, she started, looking up into the face of a young policeman. Seconds later, she realized she must look as terrified as she felt, surely a dead give-away. With tremendous effort, she forced a little laugh.

"You scared me," she said, making a face, then smiling up at him, playing for time, pretending she hadn't heard him ask for her name. She saw the patrol car now, parked at the curb a few feet away. Her mind raced, making up for the moments of complete paralysis.

The policeman returned her smile as he said again, easily, "What's your name, miss?"

"Kris." Her mind said, keep him off balance. Offer him just what he asks for, no more. If only he didn't ask for an I.D.

"Did I do something wrong?" She gestured toward the trash can. "I put my litter over there."

"Good for you." His slight amused smile was still in place, but the gray eyes studied her carefully, then glanced at the grocery bag and the tote bag beside it.

Kris saw to her horror that the rolled up towel jutted out in plain sight. And why would anybody carry a towel around with them? Unless they'd been swimming —

"Been swimming?"

She felt a surge of relief. "Yeah. Would you believe, the first time this year."

He squinted up at the sun. "Gonna be another hot one," he said. "Sure has been crazy weather. All through June, in fact, and that's when we usually freeze."

59

Just as Kris began to relax, he returned to his questions. "What's your last name, Kris?"

She had one ready. "Wilson." But what would she do if he asked for an I.D.?

He did. "Sorry to hassle you, nice day like this." He nodded at the brown paper bag. "Nice day for a swim and a picnic in the park." He sighed. "But we got a lot of runaways on the road this time of year. Way it is, we have to check out all you kids."

Kris mumbled something, pawing through her bag, pretending she couldn't find her wallet all the while she was covering one end of it with her left hand.

The radio squawked in the patrol car at the curb, and the young man turned, listened for a moment, then loped toward it. He told her over his shoulder, "Hold it a minute, will you?"

Kris watched him as she got to her feet slowly, muscles bunching in her legs, ready to run. But her luck held. After a moment, he gave her a friendly wave and the car moved down the street.

Kris let out her breath in a loud sigh and took off in the opposite direction. She had been lucky, she thought, but she couldn't depend on a minor miracle the next time someone stopped her for questioning.

She should have realized the park would be a logical place for a runaway kid to stop and rest, to eat and use the restroom. If she hadn't been aware of that fact, the cops sure had it figured out. She had better steer clear of parks after this and be grateful she had lucked out on the first dangerous confrontation. She couldn't afford a second careless mistake.

A few blocks away, she paused to shed her sweater and stow it in the tote bag. She was uncomfortably warm now, face to face with the second major difficulty of life on the road. How could she bathe?

She recalled then reading in the brochure about a KOA campground. Doubtless, that would have a washroom and showers for the campers. Nobody would pay any attention to somebody taking a shower, perhaps around noon when almost everyone was off sightseeing or having lunch. But she would need clean clothes to put on afterwards. That meant earning some money.

All afternoon, she walked around town, browsing through the Good Will store and one run by disabled veterans. Checking prices, she figured she could get underwear and a tee shirt for around a dollar. It would be wise to invest another dollar in a huge Mexican straw bag, roomy enough to carry everything she had, plus a complete change of clothes.

Briefly, she considered a zipper bag similar to the one Mindy had lent her, but she decided at last that she would look less conspicuous with the Mexican carryall. She had to keep in mind the fact that she had to lug food and clothes wherever she went. The weight and bulk of those items had to be considered.

By the time the sun hung low in the western sky, a fiery orange ball against the darkening blue, Kris found herself fighting increasing fatigue and hunger as well as the frightening, still unresolved problem of a place to sleep.

The department store seemed a good bet at first. If she hid somewhere until the doors were locked, it would offer any number of comfortable corners, she thought. Then she remembered Mrs. Kelly telling her that some of the stores in Long Beach had dogs to accompany guards on night patrol, and she discarded the idea.

At dusk, she realized she was only a few blocks from the ramp she had used that morning to come into town. Too tired to worry about the problem any more, she decided to return to the packing shed. She would be safer there than any place she had seen today.

Though her feet and legs were shaking with weariness from the miles she had walked during the past ten hours, she went down another dirt road far into the field, circling to approach the shed from the rear. She noted a few evening stars in the sky as she opened the door at last.

Relieved, she saw the packing crates still stacked against the wall. It didn't look as if anyone had been here during the day, and she guessed the shack might be one that no one used this early in the season.

It looked different to her now, neither as distasteful or frightening as it had last night. Now, it offered sanctuary. The walls gave her the first feeling of complete safety and total privacy that she had experienced all day. She could relax and let her tension drain away. Nobody would be watching her, studying her, puzzling over the way she looked or wondering about the things she carried.

For a long time, she rested, her back against the packing crates, shoes off so she could massage her tired feet and her right hand where the one handle of the tote bag had bitten deep. After a while, she ate a sandwich, washing down the dry bread with juice from the segments of an orange.

It would be so great to stand in a hot shower, she thought dreamily, and steam away her aching weariness, to wash the stickiness of perspiration off her body and shampoo her hair in an ocean of lather, to brush her teeth and hop into a fresh clean bed and —

Now, just stop that! she told herself in a fierce whisper. Only one day on the road, and here she was daydreaming about a bath, whimpering like a two-year-old. Things would work out, but she would have to toughen up to see they did.

That meant working up enough physical

stamina for ten-mile-a-day hikes. But she would have to watch her attitude, too, never for a moment allowing herself to indulge in the poor-me miseries. Now, she needed sleep so desperately, she couldn't think straight about anything.

Stretched out with the towel under her head, it seemed as if she stepped instantly into a dream about Mindy. Her friend was wearing the pink blouse, but Kris hardly recognized it. There were spots down the front, a stain on the right cuff, a jagged rip under one arm.

"You can keep it," Kris told her in the dream. "I sure don't want it back. I don't need it anymore."

Chapter
Six

She was never sure exactly what wakened her, the sound of voices or the creak of the door as it swung open. Luckily, she had been sleeping in the corner, a few feet now from the wedge of light. She shrank back, closer to the packing crates, her heart hammering against her ribs.

"You and your lousy ideas," a man's voice said, heavy with disgust. "I ain't spendin' another night in this stinkin' hole. I told you last time, Beans — "

Someone retorted in a nasal whine. "I told you, didn't I? It's my rotten sinuses, man. Every time I bed down in the open, I tell ya they kill me all the next day."

The door swung wider. Breath caught in her throat, Kris stared at the pattern of light, a bulky silhouette in the center.

"Always bellyachin' about your lousy sinuses," the first voice said, angry now. "Rotten nose of yours. Nothin' in it *but* sinuses, hear you tell it."

The whine again, bitter. "Easy for you to talk. Easy for you to say. Big man with the chicks, huh? You'd find us a place tonight. Sure. You knew a dozen chicks'd be beggin' us to — "

"Stuff it. Is it my fault she got herself a guy looks like a gorilla? King Kong, that's who old Linda latched onto. Not a brain in her whole skull, the dumb — "

"Yeah, yeah. You said all that already. A dozen times you told me. I got a headache, listening."

A pause. Feet shuffled. The silhouette vanished briefly as a match flared.

Kris caught a whiff of cigarette smoke. She lay with her arms wound tightly around her chest, as if she were trying to squeeze herself into a tiny, invisible ball.

"So all right," the whine continued. "You got any better ideas? I'm still waitin' to hear your brilliant thoughts. I ain't particular. Any place that ain't outside. I told ya — "

"Like a broken record, you told me. Okay, we're a mile from the wreckin' place. Nice soft bed in the back of a — well, for you, Beans, we'll find a Caddy. Or a late-model Lincoln Continental." The words were spaced and underlined with sarcasm. "All the windows workin' perfect, so the night air don't bother that rotten nose of yours!"

The other voice swore, a lengthy litany reflecting more of weariness than any stronger emotion. "Just so it ain't outside."

The door closed. Voices and footsteps receded. After a long moment, Kris breathed again in great sobbing gulps. She sat up and rocked back and forth, trying to control the shuddering whimpering sounds. And still she hugged herself, as if to comfort.

She had held Greg like that when he had the measles. He had been delirious before she got his fever down with aspirin and sponge baths.

No, don't think about home, she told herself fiercely. You'll go into hysterics like an eight-year-old. *Don't panic.* You haven't anybody to depend on but you. So start thinking.

A narrow escape, another lesson learned. Stupid to think of this place as a sanctuary. If Clip figured it for a good place to crash, a dozen other people could come to the same conclusion.

Tomorrow night, she would have to come up with a really ingenious idea, some place even that friend of Beans with his brilliant thoughts would never consider.

Would she be safe here for the rest of the night? She pondered the problem for a moment. It must be quite late. Chances were, nobody else would be looking for a place to sleep. She simply had to gamble. If she left at this hour, she'd be too conspicuous, in infinitely greater danger.

She found it impossible to get back into sound sleep again, though she dozed fitfully, forcing herself to relax. She needed the rest. Tomorrow would be another long, difficult day with so much to do, so many things to plan.

At first light, she roused to eat some of her food, comb her hair, and get her bags ready to leave. When she saw signs of increasing traffic on the freeway, she slipped out of the shed and headed for town.

Deliberately, she chose another service station to wash and brush her teeth. It wouldn't be wise, she thought, to be seen too often in the same places, to arouse any curiosity.

Today she had to try to earn some money, and the residential section a few blocks from the business district looked like a good place to start. The homes there were modest, but well kept up, lawns and shrubbery neatly trimmed.

Choosing at random, Kris turned into a driveway, took a deep breath as she approached the door and rang the bell.

After several moments, a young woman answered. She clutched at the front of a blue bathrobe, and her hair was tousled. From the back of the house, a baby wailed. The voices of older children quarreled shrilly.

"Yes?" the woman said, eyes and voice impatient.

"Do you have any cleaning jobs?" Kris asked and went on quickly to forestall a blunt refusal. "Windows to wash? I do a good job cleaning kitchen cupboards, too. Or ovens or refrigerators or — or shower stalls?" She forced a nervous smile. "Most people really hate cleaning shower stalls."

The young woman sighed, ran her fingers through her hair, and turned to yell over her shoulder, "Knock it off, you kids!"

She said at last, looking at Kris soberly, "You tempt me. But not today. I got my sister's kids to watch. Monsters, both of them." She hesitated, then murmured, "You do ovens? You earning money for clothes or something, honey?"

"Right." It was the truth, Kris thought grimly.

"Well, like I said, today's up for grabs. If you want to come back tomorrow, the next day — " She shrugged. "Okay?"

Kris thanked her and went on to the next house with renewed optimism. But she had no luck with anyone else on that block. On the other side of the street, she found a job at the very first house.

"Windows!" The stout middle-aged lady groaned. "Mine are so dirty, I can't tell for sure if the sun is shining. My regular boy quit me." She looked at Kris doubtfully. "Will you do a good job? How much are you charging?"

"I'll do a great job," Kris assured her, then swallowed hard. "A dollar an hour?"

Faded blue eyes narrowed, studying her. "You don't have any equipment like my boy did. If you use my things, seems only right you shouldn't charge as much." A pause. "Seventy-five cents? That seem fair?"

It didn't, but Kris was in no position to argue. "All right," she said wearily.

By two o'clock that afternoon, every window in the small house sparkled. Kris massaged her aching arms as she finished polishing the last one. It had been a long, dirty job, but the thought of the money she needed so desperately kept her going.

The woman allowed her to eat her lunch at the small kitchen table, offering lemonade and cookies to go with the sandwich Kris made.

"That'll be your tip," the lady said with a chuckle. "Sorry, I don't have any milk in the house."

"Oh, this is fine, thanks." She had never been so thirsty for a glass of cold milk, Kris thought. Funny how she had taken so many little things for granted before.

She noted the woman glance at the clock and guessed she would deduct the twenty minutes from her working time. Her guess proved correct. An hour later, she left with three dollars and a quarter in her pocket.

She was nearly positive the amount was short by fifty cents, but somehow she couldn't bring herself to argue the point. No wonder her regular boy had "quit her," as the woman put it.

Still, during the hours at the little house, Kris made an important discovery. She had been taken to a shed in the back yard to get the scrub pail and rags she needed for her job.

Closing the door, the woman glanced over the fence at the next yard and clucked with disapproval. "Look at that grass, would you? They'll be gone another week. Now, why couldn't they have hired someone to keep the place up?"

Kris thought wryly, *because they're probably a couple of nickel-nursers like you are, lady*. Then she took a closer look at the next yard and saw a large garden swing covered with some kind of shiny chintz material. There was a fringed top on it, and the swing faced the yard on the other side, one surrounded by a high redwood fence.

Safe and private, Kris thought. She could come in through the alley after dark. It would be a perfect place to sleep if she were careful not to be seen coming and going. The problem of a bed would be solved for a week, at least.

When she left, she circled to check out the alley so she would be able to locate the gate in the dark. A few minutes later, she made another discovery. At the end of the alley, she saw the rear of a supermarket, trash bins in an area next to the loading dock.

An elderly couple were bent over one of the bins, and Kris looked at them with mild curiosity as she approached. They seemed to be ordinary looking people, not too well dressed, but not shabby either. As she came closer, she saw the woman take a head of lettuce from the bin, peel off a few outer leaves and pop it in the bag the old man held for her.

Kris stopped a few feet away. She had never thought too much about the way store people might dispose of produce that was no longer fresh. There must be a lot of food that would be edible, even overly ripe fruit past the first bloom.

The old woman turned, and her face went rigid when she saw Kris watching her. "It's perfectly good food," she said, her tone defensive. "Living on a fixed income, you have to make every penny count."

"I know." Kris smiled at her. "I — we're having problems, too. That lettuce looked good. Is there any more?"

The woman's face softened. She reached into the bin, rummaged around for a moment, then brought out another smaller head.

"There you are. That'll crisp up real nice." She turned. "Come on, Dad. Just one more stop."

She began to walk away. Then she stopped to say quietly to Kris, "Try Safeway in the next block. It's a good place for fruit."

Kris took her advice, then went to a service station nearby to wash the lettuce and the peaches and nectarines she had salvaged, ripe and bursting with juice. There were small brown spots on the discarded fruit, but otherwise it was perfectly good food, as the old woman had insisted. Kris ate some of it and put the rest in a plastic bag. Then she headed for the other side of town to buy some clothes and a big straw bag.

It was a long ten block hike back to the KOA campground on the northern end of town. Kris came into it late that afternoon, but she realized at once that it was a good time of day to get her shower. There were few people around, only a couple of women beginning preparations for an early evening meal. No one paid any attention to Kris as she walked through to the shower room. She found herself holding her breath, not because she was scared, but because the smell of steaks on the barbecue racks was almost more than she could bear.

As tired as she was, she stayed under the lukewarm spray for a long time, soaping her hair twice and rinsing it well. Then she turned the warm water off to grit her teeth and endure icy cold needles that made her blood race through her body.

Never had a shower felt so refreshing. She

dressed quickly in clean clothes, then found a sunny place on a picnic bench where she could dry her hair, spreading the towel and washcloth to dry, as well.

At a table a short distance away, she watched a man playing cards with three kids, two boys about ten and a girl close to her own age. There were occasional bursts of laughter from the group. Once the man reached over to hug the girl, still chuckling as he called something to a woman bent over a camp stove nearby.

Kris looked away quickly, cross at herself because she felt tears in her eyes. What would it be like to be part of a family like that? Why had things gone so terribly wrong with her own family?

She pushed the thoughts aside and got out her food, feasting on lettuce and peaches, so hungry she didn't mind the dry bread in her sandwich. It was filling, she thought, and her spirits rose. It felt so good being clean again, knowing where she was going to sleep that night. But as she lay back on the bench, drowsily contemplating the sky, questions began to circle in her mind. What was she going to do when it rained, when the weather turned cold? It was time to plan beyond the next twenty-four hours, to figure out just how she was going to survive.

For some reason, Regan's nice ordinary face popped into her mind. He'd been so great. Should she try to call him? He had come down to visit his uncle and aunt in San Diego, he said. She remembered once that he had grinned a little sheepishly and told her he had been named for his uncle, his father's older brother. What was that nutty first name of his? O'Shaughnessy? O'Flaherity? O'Flannery, that was it.

Well, if worst came to worst, maybe she'd call him. She couldn't tell about that uncle, though, just because Regan liked him. He might be the type to turn her in after five minutes' conversation. You couldn't tell about other people's families. It would be wise right now if she didn't trust anybody.

At the edge of dark, Kris crept into the backyard with the swing, reaching over to unhook the little gate off the alley, opening it an inch at a time until she was sure the hinges wouldn't squeak.

The swing seemed blissfully comfortable after her hard bed of the last two nights, and she dropped off to sleep almost at once. She recalled turning over only a couple of times in the night.

At dawn, she lay on her side, facing the tall redwood fence.

She came awake with the same abrupt jolt that she had felt last night when she heard the voices. An invisible fist slammed into her stomach, cutting off her breath. Somehow, she sensed a presence before she opened her eyes, when she was still half asleep.

A huge black dog stood beside the swing looking at her, eyes on a level with hers. She heard a low rumble deep in his throat, and his ears were pricked forward. Obviously, he was trying to make up his mind about her. Yellow-green eyes stared at her, alert for the smallest movement.

Kris lay very still.

"Hello, boy," she said in a soft, even voice. "Where did you come from? What's your name?"

She spoke to him for several minutes, gently, calmly, watching his ears closely until it seemed to her that his tension had eased. Slowly, she extended the back of her hand for the dog's inspection. He sniffed, then sat down, still looking at her.

Carefully, Kris lowered her hand, groping for the straw bag beside the swing. She found her last piece of cheese and fed it to the dog, bit by bit. Jeb had loved cheese. Of course this dog wasn't anything like Jeb. Still, they were friends by the time she heard a whistle far down the alley, and the dog leaped over the gate and disappeared.

It had been nice visiting with him. She realized how lonely she had been for some kind of companionship. Still, she hoped he wouldn't come back. She might feel a lot safer at night with a big dog around, but if his owner came looking for him, she might well be discovered.

Slowly, she sat back on the swing. She

couldn't risk going back to sleep. It was almost time to leave. Her third day. Abruptly, she felt her stomach tighten with apprehension. She had learned a great deal in the last couple of days. She would be as careful as she could, never letting her guard down for a moment.

But was that enough? Was her luck about to run out?

Chapter Seven

After she had eaten some fruit for her breakfast, she walked to a laundromat to wash the clothes she had worn for two days. It seemed a shame to spend the money for a small load, but she couldn't wear the same grimy clothes, either, without attracting the kind of attention she wanted to avoid. And nobody would hire her for any kind of job looking so grubby, she thought.

There were only two women in the laundromat at that hour. One of them sat engrossed in a magazine while the other scolded three lively toddlers as they poked curiously into every corner.

Waiting for her things to dry, Kris studied

the cards on a small bulletin board. Among the notices was a printed ad for a family employment agency listing jobs for teenagers. Babysitters, yard workers, and mothers' helpers wanted, the ad said.

Kris sat down to check her city map and found the address of the agency clear across town, as she had suspected. She always seemed to be miles away from the place she wanted to go. At this rate, she would have to buy another pair of tennies soon.

She had worn her oldest shoes and clothes when she left home, something she now regretted though it had seemed wise at the time. How could she have known that Mindy would rip off everything she had packed in the zipper bag?

Don't think about that, she told herself firmly. She had salvaged enough to get by. But it was time to plan for the future, and she should get over to the employment agency this morning. Already it was late in the season to be applying for a summer job.

With a shock, she realized that tomorrow would be the Fourth of July. Stores would be closed. She'd have to consider that when she stopped to get food today.

The sun was already uncomfortably warm when she came out onto the street. She would be ready for a shower long before late afternoon, Kris thought, and sighed as she shifted the straw bag to her left hand.

There seemed to be dozens of kids downtown today, groups of girls giggling as they paused to look in store windows, barefoot couples walking hand in hand. They all had a place to go with families who cared about them —

Stop it! Don't think about things like that. So blasted sorry for yourself. How do you know they don't have problems even worse than yours? At least, nobody's yelling at you, telling you what to do any more, nagging when you do something wrong.

One of the girls reminded her of Patsy, though her hair was short and shiny clean. Kris pretended to look at the display of bikinis on the blank-faced mannequins as she studied the girl. What was it about her? The sullen eyes, the full, drooping mouth?

Poor Patsy. She had a lot to learn. Maybe it would be rough on her right now, shouldering the jobs that Kris had always done, but she'd be better off in the long run. When she had other people to think about, other things to consider besides her own needs and interests, she might grow up in a hurry. She could be nice when she wanted to, a good kid actually, but it had never been important to her to show her best side to anyone but her mother.

Mother.

Kris hurried on. She found the employment agency at last, a sign in the window of a small brown bungalow close to the sidewalk.

Inside, a lady sat at a battered desk in what had once been the living room of someone's home. Two file cabinets stood against one wall, and three chairs faced the desk as if the woman had been presiding at some kind of meeting.

She looked up and smiled as Kris came in, a small birdlike woman with short gray-brown hair and very bright black eyes. There were two spots of color across her cheekbones, and her thin lips were a slash of crimson. Kris noticed the lipstick had smeared a little on her upper lip.

"Hi, honey, looking for a job? Do you know, you're in luck? I just got two calls for mothers' helpers. Afternoons, one to five. Interested?"

Kris sat on the edge of the chair that the lady indicated with a wave of one thin hand. "Uh — yes, I am," she said, a little taken aback by the rapid flow of words. "What's the — what's the usual procedure?"

The lady leaned back, beaming at her, but the bright eyes studied her closely at the same time. "Oh, the standard routine," she said in her high brisk voice. "You make out a form. Experience, that sort of thing. We do like a couple of references for you girls, too. You can understand — " She coughed, a soft tactful sound.

Kris's heart sank. She should have known it wouldn't be that simple, she thought.

"I didn't realize — " She took a deep breath. She hated to lie. It made her feel dirty, some-

81

how. Besides, it just led to trouble, because anyone who lied got caught sooner or later, trapped in the third or fourth lie when they didn't match the first or second.

If it ever got easy to lie, she thought, she would be well on the way to turning into someone like Mindy.

"I'm just here for the summer," she said at last.

The lady nodded. "Well, we'll see what we can work out. Could I see some I.D.?"

Kris hesitated, then brought out her wallet and handed over the ASB card from school. She felt the hot blood in her cheeks as the woman examined it, taking her time about it.

"Long Beach? You'll be going back — when?" She opened a drawer, shuffled some papers at one side of it, made a notation on one of them. She took out a pencil before she closed the drawer.

There were a dozen pencils in a holder on top of the desk. Kris felt her stomach tighten. Was it her imagination, or had there been a subtle change in the woman's manner? What had she written on that slip of paper in the drawer?

"When school starts," she said, her mouth dry.

"Mmm." The woman smiled briefly, returned her card. "Well, I suppose we'll have to leave it up to the ladies who might hire you, right?

And of course you could bring a note from — who did you say you're staying with for the summer?"

Kris said slowly, reluctantly, "My aunt. It's on Glover Street. I don't remember the number. Florence Kelly," she added, as if the true name of the neighbor in Long Beach might diminish the size of the lie. "Mrs. Russell Kelly."

The woman wrote it down on a slip of paper. Her smile didn't touch the black probing eyes. "We've had to make a rule about you kids from out of town," she said in the quick smooth voice. "Sometimes it happens that — your plans change. It's been our experience too often that you don't stay on the job. I mean, long enough to make it worthwhile for us to place you."

Kris waited.

"I hope you understand our position. It just isn't worth our time and trouble unless we charge a small fee. A registration fee."

Kris said through stiff lips, "How much?"

"Five dollars." The bright eyes seemed to search for a reaction. "It's higher for the boys, of course." Another flash of the phony smile revealed a smudge of lipstick on one of her small pointed teeth. "Boys make more money when they stay on the job. With you girls, five dollars seems fair."

"Does it?" Kris said coldly. Another rip-off, she thought. A wave of anger rose inside until she could feel its heat in her face. She saw it reflected in a sudden flush on the woman's thin cheeks.

Her black eyes narrowed. "I don't know what you mean."

"You know very well what I mean." The words came faster now as if impelled by the force of her growing outrage. "You make your rules to fit the people who come in here, don't you? Maybe you adjust that registration fee, too."

"Look, I don't have to take any lip from your kind, girl."

"My kind? What kind am I?" Shaking, Kris could barely control her voice. "You took a good look, didn't you? Added it up with I.D. from out of town, and what did you get?" With enormous effort, she forced a laugh and thought, surprised, it sounded almost normal.

The woman stared at her, thin lips parted.

"I can guess what you thought, what *kind* you figured I was. A runaway, maybe? Even if it turned out I was telling the truth about my aunt, I wouldn't be in town long enough to make trouble for you. Because of your little under-the-table *registration fees.*"

Two spots of color stood out even more clearly on the woman's cheeks. "Trouble?" she said uncertainly. "I don't know what — "

"Stop saying that! You do know what I'm talking about. It's what you don't know that's going to make you sorry you ever thought of your rotten little con game."

She got to her feet and pointed at the desk. "That lady — you wrote her name down — Mrs. Florence Kelly — she used to work for a government agency. And if *I* don't know who to call to report you, well, you can bet she'll know."

She picked up her bag and headed for the door. Slowly, unhurried, she reached for the knob, then turned to say over her shoulder as if in afterthought, "How much you want to bet? Five dollars seem fair?"

Several blocks away, Kris ducked down an alley and found herself eventually on a side street that looked familiar. Then she recalled that it led to the library. She could sit in a corner and pretend to read a magazine while she rested and calmed down a little. Almost everything she had told that woman was the truth, but she couldn't find any comfort in that, nothing to temper her anger.

It was early afternoon before she emerged into the glare of the sunlight. It had taken at least an hour before her heart slowed its wild pounding. She had been unable to read a word of the magazine she selected. Her mind still reeled in frantic, futile circles.

What was she going to do? Where could she go?

Call Regan, she thought at last, and felt a

sudden aching hunger to hear his slow, dry voice. She had to talk to someone, somebody who cared about her. He had warned her about hitchhiking, hadn't he? He had told her not to do anything crazy. He cared a little, anyway.

She headed for a gas station and at the public phone, thumbed quickly through the R's in the book. A vast relief spread through her when she found an O'Flannery Regan listed with a San Diego number.

The woman who answered the third ring sounded cheerful and friendly. "You're from Long Beach? Oh, honey, I'm so sorry. The boys have gone to Sea World. No, I don't expect them back till around five. Could I have him call?"

"No," Kris said, so disappointed she could hardly talk. "No, I — I'll call back. Thank you."

"Oh, you do that. He'll be so sorry he missed you. Try again between five and six. What was the name?"

Kris hung up, hoping the lady would think she hadn't heard the last question. It made her feel terrible, being rude to such a nice warm voice.

She wandered aimlessly through the stores and stopped at a Dairy Queen to eat at one of the outside benches. She must buy more food, she thought, but it didn't seem important anymore. She was vaguely aware that something had happened to the mechanics of her thinking during the past few hours. She couldn't seem to plan ahead further than that phone call to Regan.

Her mind skittered restlessly, her body rigid with tension. When someone glanced at her, she felt a surge of panic. Blocks away from the Dairy Queen, a police car passed, slowing for a light, and she had to battle the urge to run.

At sundown, she had her shower at the campground. While she was drying her hair, she counted her money. It came to a little under two dollars.

She would have a hamburger and milk for dinner, she thought. She knew it was foolish to spend the money, and decided to do it anyway. She was hungry for meat, warm food, thirsty for milk. She'd get through tomorrow somehow. Now she needed to go to an outdoor place and sit close to people, listen to them talk and laugh, and pretend she was part of a group of friends. She needed that feeling.

When she located a likely hamburger stand, she saw a public phone on the sidewalk nearby. Her depression lifted in that moment. She felt unreasonably cheered by the thought that she could leave that number and wait for Regan's call while she ate. Perhaps he was home by now.

He was not, but the cheerful voice sounded glad to hear hers.

"Honey, they'll be here any minute, I'm sure. If you could leave your number?"

Kris gave it, swallowing the lump in her throat. She ordered her food and went to sit at the bench closest to the sidewalk phone. At the next table, a pretty Japanese girl talked intently to her boyfriend, their heads close together.

Gradually, Kris became aware of two boys at another table who were watching her, sharing low-voiced comments, then loud harsh laughter.

She turned away from them, a knot of uneasiness in her stomach. Now she barely tasted the food she had been so hungry for a short time ago. *Why didn't Regan call?*

One of the boys called over to her. "Lonesome? Come on over. We're buying." When Kris ignored them, their comments became cruder, their laughter more uninhibited.

The Japanese girl glanced at Kris and said something to her boyfriend. As they got up to leave, Kris froze in sudden panic. The other two family groups had already left. She couldn't stay, either, not any longer. Though it was still twilight, the streetlights had come on. It would be dark by the time she reached the backyard with the fringed swing.

As she passed the sidewalk phone, she gave it one last despairing glance, then shook her head and walked on. Traffic was sparse, and the street nearly deserted at this hour. Her steps quickened as she approached the entrance to a rundown trailer park.

Her only warning came with the sound of scuffling feet behind her. Then, as she turned, a hand came across her mouth and strong arms lifted her, hurrying her through the trailer park gate.

Recognizing the two scruffy looking boys from the hamburger stand, she struggled frantically, kicking out with both feet. As they half-dragged, half-carried her along the dark aisle close to the fence, she felt the helpless, hopeless terror of nightmare.

Unable to make any sound other than the muffled strangled scream in her throat, it seemed in those few dazed seconds that someone should hear that scream, all the same. It filled her chest, rang in her ears, a sobbing passionate surge of sound.

Help me! Please, somebody help me!

Suddenly, incredibly, a girl's voice called from the gate behind them. "Hey, wait for me! You guys, will you wait a minute?"

The sound of running feet. Again, the girl's voice called to them to wait. Kris felt herself flung to one side, and she rolled across the asphalt, banging her head against a low curb. She lay for a moment, panting for breath. When she looked up, she saw the Japanese girl bending over her.

"Are you all right?" she asked, frowning. "Don't worry, they both took off when they heard me coming. I told Mike they were after you. He went to get the guy from the stand, but I was afraid those creeps had a car back here and — " She shook her head. "Man, you really had a close call, you know it?"

Kris sat up. She could only manage a nod. Still gulping for breath, she found herself shaking uncontrollably. When she regained her voice, it was in a sound close to a sob. "Thanks."

The Japanese boy ran toward them then, followed by a young man whose white cap and jacket bore the insignia of the food chain. The girl waved them on in the direction Kris's assailants had taken, but a few minutes later as she was helping Kris to her feet, they returned, shaking their heads.

"Gone," the Japanese boy said. "A dozen places they could have ducked into — or over the fence. You okay?" he asked Kris.

She nodded once more.

"Well — " The other young man looked uncertain. "I better be getting back. You wanta call the police or something?"

"No!" The word emerged with too much force. Kris tried to smile. "No, I'm — I'm fine. Really. I'm okay."

He shrugged and went off in a loping run.

"I'm Teri Tanaka," the girl said, brushing at Kris's smudged tee shirt. "This is Mike Nogato." She grinned at him. "The Great Unbeliever, that's Mike."

He laughed a little sheepishly. "Listen," he said to Kris, "this one sees Mafia guys and CIA agents everywhere we go. So she's right one time. She'll never let me forget it." As they approached the gate, he nodded at the straw bag standing just inside. "That belong to you?"

Kris sighed, a long tremulous sound. "Yes. All my worldly goods, you might say."

He exchanged a glance with Teri. "You need some coffee," he said. "Something to steady your nerves. Hey, you're shaking all over. You're okay now. Everything's all right."

Kris went with them back to the bench she had left only a few short minutes before. She shuddered, accepted a paper cup of coffee gratefully and sipped it, promptly burning her tongue.

"I haven't really thanked you," she said at last. "I'm — Kris Wilding." After what they had done, the least she could do was give them her right name, she thought. "I'm sure glad you came along."

Mike gestured airily. His dark eyes studied her for a moment. "You need a place to crash?" His voice was casual. When she did not respond, he went on. "You live around here? Ever hear of our place?"

Bewildered, Kris shook her head.

"He doesn't mean the place where we live," Teri said with a laugh. "That's what they call the local crisis house. Our Place. It's just a big old house where the kids go to shoot pool or play cards or rap. They've got counselors, too. You know. If you've got problems — "

Kris stiffened. "I don't want to talk about —
my problems, not to anybody. I'm sorry. I know
you're trying to help, but — "

"So, okay," Mike said. "They can fix you
up with a place to sleep tonight. In the morning, you can decide what you want to do.
Sound good?"

Reluctantly, Kris agreed. She had never felt
so tired. She had walked too far and eaten
too little today, and her narrow escape in the
trailer park had left her shaken and close to
tears.

"Thanks for the coffee," she said softly.
"Thanks for everything."

They were half a block down the street
when she heard the sidewalk phone ring. She
stopped and turned to look at it, then went
on with Mike and Teri. She was in no condi-
tion now to talk to Regan.

Chapter
Eight

Our Place was in the midst of the business district, an old two-story frame house set well back from the street. Kris followed Teri and Mike up the drive and through the front door. She had finally stopped shaking, but inside she felt a numb, hopeless emptiness. She couldn't seem to care very much what happened to her now.

In memory, the past three days seemed an endless ordeal culminating in the terror of those moments in the dark corner of the trailer park. She felt drained, unable to feel even mild curiosity as she stood in the entry hall, glancing around her.

The rooms on either side were sparsely furnished with faded, shabby couches and chairs. There were only a few small threadbare rugs on the dark scarred floors.

On one of them, three girls sat playing cards. Across the hall, several boys were engrossed in a game of pool under an old-fashioned low-hanging chandelier. As Kris went with her new friends down the long hall, the girls looked up briefly, then returned to their card game. The boys didn't glance at them as they walked by.

At the back of the house across from a darkened kitchen, Teri stopped to knock at a door on which someone had taped a neatly lettered sign, Head Honcho.

A voice called, "Come in," and Teri stepped back to let Kris go first into a small cluttered office.

A young man with a round, amiable face rose from behind the desk to stand smiling at them. His face was framed by a halo of short bushy curls, and Kris noted that he was dressed much like the boys in the other rooms in jeans, a striped tee shirt, and well-worn black boots.

"This is Alan Norman, Kris," Teri said a little awkwardly. She glanced at the young man. "Kris — she needs a place to sleep tonight. But I think — I think she needs to talk to somebody. Mike and I thought — we figured you could help."

The young man stuck out his hand. "Glad to meet you, Kris." His grasp was warm and firm. "I'm a good listener, they tell me. How about a coke first?" He reached in his pocket for some change. "Teri, you want to prime the pump? I'll buy the first round."

"Nothing for us, thanks." Teri sounded relieved. "I'll get a couple for you, but Mike and I better be on our way. My mom — she'll be wondering where we are."

When she returned with the cokes, she scribbled something on a slip of paper and handed it to Kris. "That's my phone number. When you — if you get squared away, call me, why don't you? Mike and I, we'd sure like to know that you're okay."

"Thanks," Kris said from the depths of the strange numb feeling. She forced a smile. "Thanks for everything. You've been really great."

It was as if someone else were speaking through her, she thought, and she listened to the stranger's voice from a dark corner of herself, from the place where she hid, cold, afraid, alone. So terribly alone.

"Good luck." Mike grinned. The door closed behind them.

The young man sat for several minutes in easy silence.

Kris roused at last to say uncertainly, "I guess I — I don't know where to begin, Mr. Norman."

He waved a hand. "Call me Alan. Everybody's on a first-name basis around here."

She looked at him. "You don't want to know my last name?"

He smiled. "Sure, whenever you feel like telling me. Would you like to talk for a while first?" He leaned forward, hands folded on the desk in front of him. "You look like a girl who's had a pretty rough time of it. Why don't you just tell me what's been happening. I'd really like to help."

"You mean — start at the beginning?" She made a face, sipped at her coke. "It might take half the night."

"I've got all the time in the world."

It might help to talk, she thought. Maybe she could get it all straight in her head. "I live — I used to live in Long Beach," she began.

When she reached the point in her narrative where she had found herself abandoned in the packing shed, she fought tears for several minutes. It still hurt terribly to think of Mindy and the pink blouse, of her desertion.

By the time she finished, Alan had brought her another coke and a platter of homemade cookies. She didn't look at him for a long while, staring down at her hands as she spoke. Two of her nails were broken, and she thought absurdly, she'd give anything for a nail file. Why hadn't she thought to bring one along?

At last, slowly and painfully, she re-lived the horror of the moments in the trailer park. By this time, she was watching his face as he listened. The blue eyes were warm, but he showed little expression.

She said abruptly, "You aren't a person who judges people, are you? I mean, in your job, you probably hear so much, worse things than what I'm telling you — "

"Much worse," he said with a slight smile. "You've been a lucky girl, Kris. Three days on the road, two narrow escapes — no, make that three. I have a hunch you wouldn't have cared much for that commune in Imperial Beach where your friends were heading.

"But you're right, I don't judge people. I'm no good at lecturing or moralizing. All I want to do is point out your options so you can figure where you go from here. Okay?"

She nodded.

"How old are you, Kris? Fifteen?"

"Sixteen."

"Yes. And you're still in shock. You're not thinking too clearly at the moment, I know that. It would be surprising if you were after what just — almost happened to you. But tell me, where do you think you stand right now?"

"I don't know." Her voice firmed. "All I know is, I won't go home." She glared at him. "I went from the mess back there to something else just as bad. Okay, I admit that." She shuddered, a quick, cold spasm gripping her body. "I still won't go home. Isn't there something — ?"

He leaned back, his chair squawking at the

sudden movement. "That's what we're going to talk about," he said. "Your alternatives. You're sixteen, and you won't have full legal rights until you reach eighteen."

He paused to give her a wry smile. "Eighteen, the magic age. Until then, your mother or the state of California will be in charge of you. One or the other. Those are the good options. If you hit the road again, you'll get in trouble sooner or later, sure as fate. You found that out tonight."

Kris sighed under the weight of complete despair.

"If the police pick you up," Alan went on, "you'll find yourself facing the same alternatives. Your mother or the state. My job — and it's one I chose because I wanted it — is to try to straighten out your problems at home."

She shook her head, muttering into the ensuing silence, "Impossible."

"Well, then." He spread his hands. "That isn't exactly a dead end. If we can get your mother's permission, we'll place you in a foster home."

Kris stared at him. On the wall behind his desk, she saw a poster. As her mind struggled against fatigue and confusion, she read the lines on it:

Don't walk in front of me. I may not follow.
Don't walk behind me. I may not lead.
Walk beside me and just be my friend.

It was signed by someone named Camus. Nice, she thought wearily. That's what she needed, a friend. If only —

She scrubbed at her tired, burning eyes with her fists. "Do you have to — would you have to call my mother?"

"Yes." His voice said there would be no getting around that.

Kris groaned softly.

"Have you thought about what your mother may have gone through these past three days?" Alan's voice was still gentle, reflective, with no judgmental undertone. "Think about it now, honestly. You say she doesn't love you. Maybe you're right. I don't know your mother. But, Kris, you haven't said she hates you. You haven't even told me that you hate her. The two of you — and your brothers and your sister —you've just been trapped in a pretty unhappy situation. Isn't that about the size of it?"

"I suppose so," she said at last. "But what if — what if you call and ask her to give permission for — you know — a foster home — and she says no?"

She couldn't imagine her mother ever agreeing to such a thing. Not her mother, always worrying about what people might say or think. She might not care about her oldest daughter, not love her as a mother should, but she would never admit to the world that she had failed. That's what it would amount to if she allowed someone else to take charge of her child, the admission of failure.

No, Kris thought. Her mother would feel shamed, disgraced. Rather than face that, she'd insist that her daughter be returned to her, so no one would know she had been a rotten mother. That's the way it would turn out.

"You might be surprised," Alan said as if he were reading her mind. "When there's a breakdown in family relationships, I find that parents feel just as helpless, just as frustrated as you kids do, no matter who's at fault. In your case, Kris, if your mother says no to a foster home, well, we can work from there. But there's a chance she'll agree. That opens up a whole new option for both of you."

He waited in the same comfortable silence as before for several minutes.

Kris tried to brace herself for the inevitable. They couldn't send her back tonight, she thought. She needed to rest, to sleep, to get her head together. Maybe she could figure something out in the morning.

"All right," she said and gave him her name and phone number. "Could I wait outside?" She saw him hesitate and added dully, "I won't run out on you. I'm too tired to go anywhere."

He smiled. "I wasn't worried about that. I just thought you might like to talk to your mother."

Somehow Kris summoned up the energy to

tell him fiercely, bitterly, "I hope I never have to talk to her again. Ever."

She leaned against the wall outside while he placed the call, close enough to hear the rumble of his voice, far enough away so she couldn't hear what he was saying. A few minutes later, he opened the door, and she went back to sit down.

Alan was smiling. "Everything worked out fine," he said. "Your mother's agreed to a foster home for you."

Kris stared at him in disbelief. Her mind simply refused to accept the words until he repeated them.

"She's pretty upset," he told her. "She was crying so hard, it was difficult to understand her. But there won't be any problem, Kris."

He gestured. "Paperwork can wait. We'll have to get you squared away now so you can sleep in a regular bed tonight. How does that sound?"

Kris nodded, unable to find her voice, still unsure she had understood. Her mother crying? She must be in a red-hot fury. *She didn't want her back*. Her mother must actually hate her, so much that she couldn't stand having her home again, even as the household heavy.

She looked up to see Alan watching her as he spoke into the phone to someone he called Chloe.

"Good. I'll bring her right over. Hey, Chloe,

she likes your cookies. I don't have to sell her on your cooking."

He hung up and pressed a buzzer that summoned a young woman from somewhere in the house. She smiled at Kris as he told her where they were going. Then they went out the back door to his car, an ancient VW.

"You'll like Chloe," he told her as they drove through the dark streets. "She's got two other kids staying with her, a girl a little older than you, and a boy about fourteen. Chloe and Dunny — their name's Dunham — they run a tight ship. I think you'll be happy with them."

Kris said around a vast yawn, "You really help people a lot, don't you? Is Chloe's house close to your place? I mean, Our Place?"

"Just a few blocks." He turned to smile at her. "I hope you come by after you get settled in."

He turned into a driveway beside a modest stucco house with an enormous pepper tree in the front yard. As they approached the front door, it opened to reveal a small, slight, middle-aged woman with neatly clipped graying hair.

She said, smiling, "Hello, Alan. You've had a long day." Snappy brown eyes observed, accepted what they saw in one sweeping glance. "This is Kris? Welcome to the family."

Kris stepped into a small living room that seemed overly full of people and worn but comfortable furniture. A boy with shaggy hair scrambled to his feet from a spot close to the TV.

Behind him, a big blocky man reached to switch off the sound. When he rose, bright eyes squinting in a smile, Kris noted a shock of gray-blonde hair and thought, he looks like a retired sea captain.

"I'll leave you in Chloe's hands," Alan said. When she turned to thank him, he added, "*Good* hands, Kris. Stop by Our Place when you get a chance, and let me know how it's going. Okay?"

When the door closed, Chloe said briskly, "Kris, this is my husband, Dunny, and this is Fred Durbin."

The boy bobbed his head, and owlish glasses slid down his narrow nose. "Just call me Frog," he said in the gravelly voice that must have earned him the nickname.

"Frog," Kris murmured, thinking it odd that he didn't seem to mind a name like that.

"Just bring your things back to your room," Chloe said then and preceded her to the hall and down to an open door at the end.

The bedroom there was just large enough to accommodate twin beds with pink quilted spreads, two chairs upholstered in white nauga-hyde, and a chest of drawers in one corner. On the wall above the chest was a large round mirror with a painted pink frame.

A girl lay propped against her pillows in one

of the beds, reading under a small gold lamp clipped to the headboard. As they came in, she sat up, and Kris had a quick impression of long, gently curling red hair, white skin, and large, dreamy gray eyes.

"This is Jilleen Cunningham," Chloe said. "Jilleen, Alan just brought you a new roommate, Kris Wilding."

The girl smiled. "Hi, Kris," she said in a voice as soft and dreamy as her eyes.

Chloe stood for a moment, looking at both girls, then gave a little nod as if she had satisfied herself about something. "Well, you'll want a nice warm bath, Kris, and something hot in your stomach. What do you have in the way of clothes, honey? Sometimes the kids come to me without a stitch beyond what they're wearing, so it won't be any problem. I have a big cupboard full of things I gather from here and there."

She spoke in short machine-gun bursts of speech, warm but with a firm no-nonsense manner that Kris found vaguely reassuring. Alan had said Chloe ran a "tight ship," she recalled.

In the moment that followed the thought, she withdrew once more into the dark inner corner of herself. No attachments, no getting involved with people who might hurt her again. No trusting anybody, she told herself firmly. She had to survive for a while. As long as she was safe and she didn't have to go back home, one place was as good as another.

Silently, she unpacked the big straw bag, laying the clean clothes on the bed, the bags of food and her towel and washcloth on the chair.

"Mmm," Chloe said, and her lower lip protruded as she considered the problem. "You're a little one, aren't you? Size 8 or 9?"

"Usually seven. Eight's okay, though." Kris shrugged. "Anything at all will be fine."

Jilleen got out of bed and went to rummage in the chest of drawers. "Here's some pajamas. It won't make any difference if they're a little big." She hesitated. "You look beat," she said then. "Why don't you — ?"

"Yes." Kris blinked at the little woman watching her. "I'm not really hungry. If I could just have a shower and — "

Chloe nodded. "Bathroom's right next door. I'll get you a towel. Anything else can wait till morning."

A few minutes later, Kris crawled into bed, grateful for the smell of clean sheets, the feeling of a mattress beneath her tired body. She would be safe tonight.

She should thank Jilleen for the pajamas, she thought drowsily. It would be wise to try and get along here. No telling how long she'd have to stay.

"Does the light bother you?"

"No," she mumbled, opening her eyes. But

they were too heavy to stay open. She had only a glimpse of Jilleen's slender arm reaching to adjust the lamp.

There was a scar on her wrist, Kris noted. Then she fell into the soft, warm nothingness of sleep.

Chapter
Nine

Kris woke at last to find the sun streaming through the bedroom window. The door was closed, the other bed empty, and she saw Jilleen's pajamas on her chair. Apparently they had decided not to disturb her, Kris thought. She stretched, still a little groggy from the night's deep, dreamless sleep.

For a few minutes, she lay thinking about the place she had come to, feeling the first stir of curiosity about these people. Frog and his harsh adolescent voice, Jilleen with the scar on her wrist, Chloe, and Dunny of the bright blue sea-captain eyes.

Well, she would be safe here, and it didn't

matter whether or not she was happy. Survive, she thought, until that magic age, eighteen. That's when the books were closed, Alan said. Almost two years, an eternity, but she would manage somehow. Anything would be better than life on the streets of this town — or any other town.

She shivered, tossed the blanket back, and dressed quickly. When she opened the door, she heard the murmur of voices in the kitchen, but she saw the bathroom was empty.

Someone had hung her towel on the shower-door rod beside a small strip of tape with her name on it. This morning she noted stickers on the two other rods, as well, one for Frog and one for Jilleen. Chloe ran a tidy ship, too, she thought with a faint amusement. Taking the hint, she went back to the bedroom after she had washed, and made her bed.

Jilleen came down the hall just as she finished. "Thought I heard you up and around," she said. "Chloe asked me to show you which drawers to use. The two on the bottom are empty. And here are the house rules." She held out a piece of paper.

Someone had printed on it, neatly: 1. What we have is to use. Pick up and clean up for the next person. 2. Five-minute limit on phone calls. 3. No going out on school nights unless it's something special. We talk about it together and decide. 4. No smoking in bedrooms. Cigarettes are not furnished.

At the bottom of the page in red ink were the words: *To love is to be loved.*

Kris read it without comment, went to put her things in the bottom drawer, then perched on the edge of her bed as she watched Jilleen make hers.

Long silky red hair fell across the girl's cheek as she bent to tuck the spread under the pillow. She looked up to smile at Kris.

"No sweat," she said. "If you've got the first-day jitters, just relax. It's a whole lot better here than where you've been, for sure."

Without thinking, Kris blurted, "Does everybody know — ?"

Jilleen shook her head. "Nobody but Chloe. I guess Alan filled her in, whatever you told him. Listen, we had one girl here who slept in a Good Will collection box for six weeks. And I was on the road for a whole year, Yuma to T.J., clear up to Seattle and down again. This place is so great after the dumps I used to flop in, they'd have to use dynamite to pry me loose."

She added casually when Kris did not respond, "Hungry? Chloe's still hitting the coffee pot out there. She doesn't wake up till her caffeine level hits a certain point."

Kris nodded and headed for the kitchen. She found the little woman sitting at a big round table, sipping from a mug labeled The Boss.

"Good morning." Chloe smiled and got to her feet. "Did you get a good night's sleep?"

"Great," Kris said politely. "Thanks for letting me sleep myself out. I guess I needed it."

The brown eyes twinkled. "I figured as much. How about some hot cereal and muffins? There's a pitcher of juice in the refrigerator." She pointed out the dish cupboards and the drawer that held silverware as she put Kris's breakfast on the table.

"We have a list of jobs on the bulletin board over there," she said then. "They're rotated every Monday. Main thing around here is sharing what we have and pitching in on the clean-up, whatever makes it easiest for the whole family."

She sat down, studying Kris with a slight smile. "Because that's what we are," she said, "a family. We care about each other in this house, and that's one thing you can count on — that we'll care about you, too."

Kris mumbled uncomfortably, "You don't even know me."

Chloe laughed. "We will in time."

"I could be a terrible person," Kris persisted as something drove her on to pursue the point.

It just seemed a dumb thing for someone to say, "We'll care about you," before they had anything to base that caring on. The same sort of thing used to bother her in Sunday School when the teacher insisted that people should love their neighbor. What if that neighbor were completely unlovable? Did you get points against you if you couldn't work up affection

110

for every single crummy person you bumped into?

"Well, if you're terrible, we'll find that out pretty quick," Chloe said, sounding amused. "Five people living in a house this size, they get to know each other in a hurry."

She paused. "I didn't say we'd grow to love you overnight. I said we'd care about you. All of you kids have problems of one kind or another. That's why you end up in a place like this. So that's what we're concerned with at first, the things that happened to you before you came."

Kris buttered a muffin as she thought about that. Before she could respond, Frog burst through the back door and skidded to a halt as he saw her at the table.

"Hi," he said and stood for a moment regarding her with unconcealed interest. "Good muffins, huh?"

Kris grinned at him and nodded.

He wore nothing but a pair of cut-off jeans, and his narrow chest and skinny legs made him look about the twins' age. Yet, Alan had said he was fourteen. Then, as he crossed the kitchen and went down the hall, she drew in her breath. There was a network of ugly scars across his back and down the pitifully thin legs.

Chloe saw the expression on her face. "His father used to beat him with just about anything handy," she said, her voice quiet. "The worst scars are the ones you can't see. But Frog's coming along real good. For a long time, you couldn't get him to take his shirt off or go around in shorts, and he wouldn't be alone with Dunny under any circumstances."

Kris finished the last few bites of muffin, though she had lost her appetite. Chloe rinsed her dishes and started the dishwasher while Kris studied the job list, deciding at last to sign up for vacuuming and dusting the house.

Following instructions, she found dustrags and the vacuum in a utility closet on the back porch. She worked her way through the living room, a small family room, the hall, and three bedrooms, picking up newspapers and magazines and an assortment of paperback books as she went.

"Stack the papers in the box on the porch for the pick-up," Chloe told her. "Magazines go in the rack. And the books will all be Frog's, I think. He's hung up on science fiction these days."

Frog appeared at the sound of his name, glasses slipping halfway down his nose. "You like *Star Trek*?" he inquired eagerly. "You ever read Bradbury or Asimov or Heinlien?"

Kris nodded. "I read a Bradbury book once. And I used to watch *Star Trek*." It seemed a dozen years ago when there had been time to read or watch TV back home in Long Beach.

What would they be doing today? Her mother would be working, of course. Holidays were busy times at the restaurant. And the twins would be playing outside, probably riding the bike they got for their birthday. She could picture Patsy sprawled on the living room couch, watching game shows or soap operas on TV. She jerked her attention back to Frog.

"I guess I've seen every one of those shows at least six times." There was a note of pride in his voice. "I really dig Spock." He added in a resonant imitation of the Vulcanite-Earthling, "Fascinating."

A little later when she was returning the vacuum to the closet, Chloe called to her to go through the clothes in the hall cupboard.

Kris found a pair of dark green shorts that fit and a yellow sleeveless blouse to go with it. Then she tried on a pair of denims that looked brand-new, and made a soft sound of disappointment when she saw they were too big around the waist.

Chloe glanced at her, then at the denims, lower lip extended. "You like those? Well, I'll just take a tuck in the waistband, maybe a couple, one on each side. No trouble at all."

Kris looked up quickly. "I could do it."

"Sure, you could, but I'll be glad to do it for you. That's my job around here, the sewing and mending." She chuckled. "We ought to put that on the list on the bulletin board. Oh, I share the cooking whenever anybody wants to try their hand. But nobody has to help if they don't care for it."

She pinned the waistband, stepped back to

study it, then gave a brief, satisfied nod. "Seems like the boys get a bigger kick out of cooking nowadays than girls do. Frog mixed up the breakfast muffins this morning. And I must say, he's getting pretty good at lasagna, too."

The bedroom door had not been tightly closed, and a large dog pushed it open at that moment to stroll in and stand looking at them, tongue lolling.

Kris felt her heart turn over. The dog might have been Jeb's twin. It even had the same unruly tufts behind its ears, and the eyes were identical, his gaze fastened on Chloe with an adoring expression.

"You never bother to knock, do you?" she told him with mock exasperation. "Kris, this is Joe, our senior citizen."

Kris stared at the dog, chewing her lip as she saw that he was indeed advanced in years. Another Jeb, she thought, ready to work his way into her heart, to make a place for himself there. And if anything happened to him, it would tear her up all over again.

She steeled herself against the possibility. "Joe?" she said with a faint smile. "Where did you come up with a name like that? So unusual, I mean."

Chloe laughed. "When I was little," she said, "I read a book called *Beautiful Joe* about a real ugly dog. But he was beautiful inside even though people were mean to him. He died in the end. Real tear-jerker. Must have broken a

114

lot of hearts in its day, I figure, if it got to a tough cookie like I was." She shook her head and muttered, "Awful book. No excuse for a book like that."

Blinking rapidly, a suspicious shine in her eyes, she bent to touch the dog's head.

A moment later, Jilleen knocked at the door, waiting for Chloe to say "Come" before she entered the room. She must have seen Kris's quizzical expression because she smiled and shrugged.

"We knock on closed doors around here," she explained, "even if it happens to be the door to our own rooms."

She sat down on the chair by her bed. "I don't know about you, but I think it's really cool when people respect privacy like that. You take communes now, there isn't a corner of a closet or a cupboard you can call your own. Crowds of people wandering in and out of your life, ripping off your food and your clothes as they go, most likely. Or other things you don't care about giving away — "

She lifted her head and laughed, tossing the long red hair back from one shoulder. "They call it sharing, but I'm here to tell you, it can be a one-sided process. Those turkeys are better on the take than they are handing anything out for free."

She glanced at the clothes on the bed and the denims Kris had slipped off to hand to Chloe. "You found something? That's good."

Chloe went out, taking the dog with her, much to Kris's relief, and closing the door behind her. Kris slipped into the shorts and blouse, aware of Jilleen's thoughtful silence. Everyone in Chloe's "family" seemed to be taking turns, she thought, trying to entertain her or attempting to draw her out, not very subtle about it, either.

She didn't want to discuss her problems, not again. Talking to Alan last night had stirred up all the pain, the anger, the old festering bitterness. What good would it do to keep reminding herself how it had hurt, to feel the same helpless frustration in an aching knot inside?

"That's cute on you," Jilleen commented in her soft voice. "It's going to be nice, having a roommate again."

Kris held her breath, hoping she wouldn't come out with that caring-about-you routine. As the other girl lifted her arms to touch her hair, she noted that there were scars on both wrists. Quickly, she turned away before Jilleen saw that she had noticed. She didn't want to hear about Jilleen's troubles any more than she wanted to talk about her own.

"I'm sure we'll get along okay," she said in a tentative voice, "but — what if you couldn't stand me? What if you knew right away with one look that you didn't want any part of a roommate like me? Would you still be stuck?"

Jilleen smiled. "No, you wouldn't stay long

in that case. Chloe lets us know beforehand when somebody new is on the way. We just give her a thumbs-up if it looks okay, or a thumbs-down if it doesn't. We don't have to give a reason."

She sat back, looking at the ceiling, her eyes placid. "She's really great, you know? Maybe some of her ideas go back fifty years, and a few of the rules seem a little weird. I figure she's entitled. When you add everything up, Chloe is one fantastic lady."

Kris perched in her own chair, bare feet tucked under her. "Weird rules?" she echoed, curious.

Jilleen rolled her eyes. "Cussing," she said. "Chloe says, 'profanity is insanity.'" She giggled. "It was a strain at first. When I'd get really uptight, up to here with purity, I'd come back to my room and close the door and sit down and say very quietly — "

In a soft uninflected voice, she rattled off a loosely connected string of words and phrases that would have done credit to a longshoreman, one with the gifts of imagery and total recall.

She looked at Kris then and added, deadpan, "I don't have to do that anymore."

Kris burst out laughing.

Looking pleased, Jilleen bounced to her feet. "We'll have time to talk later. Do you play badminton? Dunny put up this neat net out in back, but old Frog's always buried in a book — "

"I'm not very good," Kris said.

"Neither am I. Only thing I was ever any good at — well, they don't play those games in this neighborhood."

She let the cryptic remark dangle as she led the way down the hall and through the back door.

An hour later, breathless and exhausted, the two girls came in for lunch. Afterward, Kris asked Chloe if she could make a couple of phone calls. She wanted to tell Teri and Mike that she was settled in. She wanted to really thank them for rescuing her.

And Regan had been on her mind, too. If he had tried to return her call, he might be worried about her. She tried to dismiss that idea with the scorn it merited, but Regan's thin face kept popping up in her mind, all the same. And it always had a worried expression.

"Long distance?" Chloe asked, turning from the sink to look at her.

"No. Teri and Mike, the kids who — and Regan's a boy from Long Beach. He's visiting his aunt and uncle in San Diego this summer."

Chloe waved a hand. "Fine. I'll even waive the five-minute limit. But that only goes for the first day, hear?"

Kris made the calls from the phone in the family room, saving the one to Regan for last. Her heart gave a little leap when he answered. For a moment or two, she couldn't speak.

"Regan? It's Kris. Kris Wilding."

"Kris! Hey, am I glad you called! I tried to get back to you last night and — "

She sighed. "It's a long story. Maybe I'll tell you about it some day. Regan, I'm staying at this place in Chula Vista."

"A commune?" He sounded casual, uncritical.

"No. Oh, no. Mindy went on — she went on without me." She continued smoothly, hoping he wouldn't want to talk about it, "Matter of fact, I'm in a foster home."

"You are? Hey, that's great. I mean, I always thought — well, I think you'll be a lot better off without — "

"Without Mindy?" She gave a short laugh. "Yeah, I was lucky, way it turned out. So, anyway, I'll be staying here a while, I guess."

He sounded glad about that. "I could come out and see you," he suggested. "My aunt lets me use her car and — " He hesitated.

"I think it would be okay," Kris said, "if — if you want to."

"Tomorrow night? We could get something to eat somewhere and see a movie, maybe."

"Okay." Kris took a deep breath. "Could you hold on while I make sure?"

In the kitchen, Chloe nodded approval, provided Kris promised to be in at a reasonable hour. She raced back to the phone.

"Far *out*," Regan said happily. "We may even postpone the movie and just talk. We've got a lot to catch up on."

119

As she listened, Kris saw the dog, Joe, come into the room. She watched him uneasily as he came to stand a few inches away, head a little to one side, looking at her with Jeb's melting brown eyes.

For a second or two, she stared at him. Then she put out her hand and, gently but firmly, she pushed him away.

Chapter
Ten

She felt a little shy with Regan at first, though it was great to see him again, standing at the door smiling down at her as if he were really glad to see her. The evening was strange, in a way, because it seemed as if they had both grown up a lot since they met in English class a few months ago.

For one thing, Regan didn't seem uncomfortable at all as he shook hands with Chloe and Dunny and nodded at Frog grinning up at him from his favorite spot on the floor in front of the TV. Kris found herself relaxing, too, as Regan sat for a few minutes talking about the bottom-fishing he'd been doing on his uncle's small boat.

"Nice people," he told Kris when they went out to the car. "They seem like a — well, like a real family." He glanced at her as he turned the ignition key. "How's it going?"

She had forgotten what a comfortable person he was, but somehow in the brief time she had known him, one thing had registered. Even during the turmoil of the last few days, as hard as she tried to dismiss the possibility, she knew that he cared about her.

In the odd chemistry in which one person could be instantly drawn to another — or just as quickly repelled — Regan had seen something about her that he liked. Kris paused for a second or two to wonder what it could be.

She smiled at him. "It's going to be okay, I guess. Chloe keeps saying we're a family, too." She gave a brief laugh. "Maybe I just don't have any good feeling about — about being part of a family."

Regan drove slowly through the dark streets. "That's natural," he said. "You didn't have it too easy before."

She looked at him, puzzled. He seemed to know how it had been for her at home. But how could he know?

As if he read her mind, he said into the short silence, "Greg Curtis used to live next door to you. He was in my P.E. class." He turned to grin at her. "I drove him crazy, asking questions about you."

"Oh." Startled, Kris added, "Yes, I talked to him once in a while, usually over the back fence."

Regan nodded. "While you were mowing the lawn or giving the dog a bath or riding herd on about six kids. No, I don't want to embarrass you. I just wanted you to know that I figured you had a pretty good reason to cut out like you did."

He hesitated. "I felt really low, though, thinking I'd lost contact. When my aunt said you'd called, *wow!* And then — you were gone again. Promise me one thing, will you? If things ever get bad for you, will you call me? Will you let me try to help?"

Kris was silent for a moment. She had to choke back a lump in her throat before she said, "Okay, I promise. Thanks."

His smile warmed his thin face. "Good. Now that's settled, what would you like to eat? Chinese food or Mexican or Italian? Where's a good place where we can talk?

Kris gave him directions to a small family restaurant, one that specialized in Mexican and Italian food. She had asked Chloe to recommend a nice place which wouldn't be too expensive.

"It isn't a fancy place. I don't have many clothes," she told Regan a bit awkwardly. "I — I lost everything I brought from home."

He glanced at her outfit, the yellow blouse

and the denims from Chloe's cupboard. "You look great," he said. "I want to take you to Sea World and the zoo. Man, you can spend a whole day there and still not see everything. And you can wear that outfit wherever we go, okay?"

She laughed. "If you don't mind, I sure don't."

They were still making plans for the weeks ahead as they finished their dinner in the outdoor patio in back of the restaurant, gayly decorated with colorful Mexican piñatas hanging over the rustic tables.

Kris sighed happily. "This may just be the best summer I've had in — ever since I can remember."

"I hope so." His eyes were serious. "You haven't had much fun, have you? I think those people — Chloe and Dunny — they'll help you, Kris, if you let them."

She looked down at her plate. "I don't know," she said uncertainly. "Maybe there's something wrong with me. I can't seem to — to feel close to them."

It came out then in a bewildered burst of words. "They're trying so hard, too. Like yesterday, we all made a Fourth of July cake and decorated it with red, white, and blue icing and little flags on top. Dunny put up a big flag in front because it was a holiday. He used to be a sergeant in the Marines. It was Frog's turn to choose a special dinner, they said, and he wanted pizza. So we all helped with that. But why should I feel that I'm not really a part of any of it? It's like there's a wall around me, so I can't reach out to any of them."

He took her hand and held it tightly. "Because too many things have been happening to you. No, you don't have to tell me about them. But the way I see it, maybe you've been feeling too much. Maybe this is just a way of protecting yourself for a while. I mean, you don't — you don't feel like there's a wall between us, do you?"

She looked up, horrified to feel tears burning behind her eyes. "No," she said miserably and swallowed hard. Of all times to begin feeling something, to let something get through to the strange cold emptiness inside her.

Deliberately, she changed the subject to safer ground. "Your aunt sounded really nice on the phone. I felt bad, playing games with her. Along about then, I was getting pretty spacey. Paranoid, that's what I was."

He laughed, then released her hand as if he sensed her withdrawal. "You'll like her," he said. "Fantastic lady, my aunt. You'd be surprised what she picked up from your voice on the phone."

"What?" Kris asked, curious. "What did she say?"

Regan studied her for a moment with a faint smile. But his eyes were dark and still. "She said, 'Regan, that girl's in trouble. She's scared to death about something. I got a strong impression of someone very young and vulnerable, and so *frightened*. Regan, you've got to help her!' "

He drew in a breath. "Right on the money, she was. So I told her" — his voice deepened, firmed — "I told her this is a very special girl, a funny combination. She's small, but not soft and silly like a lot of little girls. Vulnerable in a different way, too, because she's strong and level-headed and intelligent. So maybe she thinks she's capable of handling almost any situation. And that could be a dangerous thing because — she can't. Not at her age, as pretty as she is, not even aware that she's pretty. She might be in big trouble, all right."

"Oh, *don't*," Kris said, tears in her voice. "Regan, don't make me cry."

He changed key instantly. "On the other hand," he said brightly, "I told her it might be another Kris — Kris Zambonavich — and she's a red-headed lady lifeguard who's been after me ever since I got here."

He looked relieved when she blinked rapidly, then grinned at him. "Let's get out of here," he said.

It had been a wonderful evening, even with the occasional low moments when all the unhappiness from the past revived to sweep over her again. Though she never did spell any of it out to Regan, the fact that disclosure wasn't necessary seemed to draw them closer. She

126

could tell that he understood, and that was the important thing.

All during the next two days, Kris found herself re-living that evening, recalling the things they talked about. *A girl who isn't even aware that she's pretty.* The words burned through her mind with a glow that brought a flush to her face each time she remembered them. Regan had said that to his aunt about *her*.

She would study her face in the bathroom mirror, wonder stirring within. She wasn't ugly, of course, and she supposed her features went together well enough. More than that, she couldn't say. Turning away with a sigh, she decided, if Regan thought she was pretty, that was enough of a miracle for her.

He had kissed her good night when he left her at the door, a gentle tentative kiss which showed plainly that he hadn't had much more experience along those lines than she had. She was glad about that. She could tell he liked her, even without the memory of his voice saying, *this is a very special girl.* She found it easy to respond, to believe what he said without having to test him in any way.

She examined that thought, a little bothered by it. Was she turning into the kind of person who had to test people before she trusted them? Yes, of course she had come to feel that way. After her experience with Mindy, her very best friend, and the people who had tried to cheat her, the lady who short-changed her after she worked so hard washing windows, the lady at the employment agency — well, after that, why wouldn't she be a little reluctant to trust people? Still, there seemed no good reason for that wariness to extend to Chloe and Dunny, and to Frog and Jilleen, as well.

The second afternoon, she walked over to Our Place to talk to Alan, admitting to herself that the cookies she had baked were an excuse to see him again. Maybe he could help straighten out her head. She had to talk to someone, and Alan was a good listener.

He rose from behind his cluttered desk with a broad grin, obviously pleased to see her. "Hey, this is great." He took the box she held out. "More of Chloe's cookies?"

Kris laughed. "No, actually they're mine. I hope you aren't disappointed. My little brothers like these, but they like anything made with peanut butter."

Waving her to a chair, he sat down to sample one.

"Fantastic! I'm prejudiced, myself, when it comes to peanut butter. Thanks, Kris. That was nice of you." Then, leaning back, he smiled at her. "Well, are you settled in? How are things going?"

"Fine," she said. "Are you busy? There's something I want to — to ask you."

"That's what I'm here for."

She fumbled for words, deciding at last she

would just describe her feelings as she had to Regan. Then she leaned forward, palms flat on the desk, watching him.

"My friend, he thought — he said that so much has been happening to me, that maybe I'd felt too much. But it worries me, you know? I don't like to feel all closed off from the people around me."

Alan nodded. "You'd like to go back to the way you were? Even if that would mean you'd risk being hurt again?"

She shook her head, a little desperate now because she didn't really know what she meant, what she wanted. She was only sure that she felt miserable, isolated, alienated, set apart.

"Emotion can be a dangerous thing," he said, his blue eyes thoughtful. "But the human animal has to deal with a lot of things that have an element of danger. It's a matter of learning control, judgment. I would think it could be far more uncomfortable to block normal emotion. If that lessens the possibility of further pain, well, it also precludes feeling joy and love and the warmth of closeness with friends. Right?"

"Yes," Kris said after a moment. She found her gaze wandering to the poster on the wall. *Walk beside me and just be my friend.*

"You like that poster?" Alan opened the double drawer at one side of his desk. "I have some copies. A lot of the kids seem to respond to Mr. Camus." He handed her a smaller version, rolled up and secured with a rubber band.

"Let's talk about his philosophy for a minute, Kris. What do you think he's trying to say?"

Kris took a deep breath, then let it out in a noisy sigh. "It would be scarey to lead," she said slowly, "especially if you weren't sure you were heading in the right direction. No, I wouldn't want to lead anybody, not now, anyway. I'm not sure of anything anymore."

She wouldn't want to follow, either, she thought. That was the main reason she had left home, wasn't it? Because of her mother dragging her along, telling her what to do, never listening, never showing any love, never thanking her or praising her, never doing anything a mother should.

She told Alan some of that, then stopped, lips pressed together, when she heard the bitterness in her voice, the harshness of anger.

"Don't hold it in," he said gently. "If those are your feelings, be honest about it. Take them out and look at them. The only thing I'd suggest is that you try to see the situation from your mother's viewpoint, too."

He held up his hand when he saw her expression tighten. "I'm not saying that what she feels is valid, or that she's acted wisely. I'm merely pointing out that she has a right to her feelings just as you do.

"It would be great if you could learn to understand what she's done, the reasons she acted as she did. I mean, if you can see her, not as your mother, but as a human being, flawed as we all are flawed — Kris, if you can manage that, you'll be well on your way to growing up. And to becoming a far better happier person, at that."

She said stiffly, "You're asking me to forgive her?"

"Your word, not mine." He gave her a cheerful grin. "I just want you to think about what I've said. We don't impose any penalties around here or set any time limits. All we want to do is help you straighten out those knots inside that are making you so uncomfortable."

He added, his voice quiet, "The scientists are learning more every day about the physical damage that corrosive emotions can do. Things like hate and anger and bitterness chew you up inside. But if you take tolerance and understanding in equal parts, it's the best antidote in the world."

In a quick change of mood, he held out the box. "Have a cookie," he urged, "and tell me what you think of Chloe and her household."

Kris nibbled at a cookie without enthusiasm. "They're all really nice. I guess I — I just wish I could feel closer to them. Frog's like a friendly puppy, tagging around at Dunny's heels. And Jilleen — " She glanced up at Alan. "She must have gone through a lot on the road. A whole year she was gone, she said. I noticed the scars on her wrists."

He nodded. His eyes narrowed for a moment as he stared at the pencil holder on his desk.

"Jilleen met some pretty rough people in her travels. It's one reason I told you it might have been a stroke of luck, the way you were abandoned by your friend before you got to that place in Imperial Beach. The idea behind communal living isn't bad, you know, but unluckily the greatest ideas have to be put into action by people. With varying degrees of success."

He brooded for a second or two, then shrugged. "Jilleen opted out, once she'd been thoroughly disillusioned. She made a few half-hearted attempts at suicide, then one that almost worked."

He looked at Kris. "Ask her about it some time. She's quite open about her experiences, comes down here to rap with the kids, as a matter of fact. Says it helps her come to terms with that year on the road. Quite a girl, Jilleen."

Kris stirred. He would ask her about Chloe next, she thought, and what would she say? She must be really gutless to be scared to care about someone, to be afraid that despite all the evidence to the contrary someone was simply too good to be true.

At the employment agency, she had felt a deep shame when she lied. She remembered thinking at the time, was it worth it, taking the chance she could turn into someone like Mindy? Instead, she had become suspicious and fearful, full of the corrosive emotions Alan had mentioned.

Except for the way she felt about Regan.

She got up from her chair and headed for the door. "Thanks for listening," she said. "It helped. And — I'll think about what you said." She hurried down the hall before he had a chance to ask about Chloe.

Hold onto the thought of Regan, she told herself. She had one person she could care about and trust. Maybe some day there would be others.

Chapter
Eleven

Dunny had already left for work when Kris came to the breakfast table that morning. She helped herself to juice, scrambled eggs, and toast, and slid into her chair.

Chloe smiled at her, rolling her eyes as she nodded toward Jilleen and Frog. The two were engaged in a spirited exchange about the merits of a movie they had seen on TV.

"Dumb chick, she was asking for trouble," Frog declared in a voice heavy with disgust. "Mixing in with characters like that. What'd she leave home for in the first place? I didn't see anybody beating on her, did you?"

Jilleen brushed her hair back from her face. "There can be other reasons to split," she said, her tone gentled by her smile. "You have to admit, nobody was on her wavelength. But she had to find out for herself that she was better off at home than those places she landed in later on. Frog, that was real life you were watching."

He brooded, staring into his juice glass. "Who wants movies about real life?" he muttered. "That isn't what I watch movies for. Maybe a lot of people'd rather not be reminded about real life." He gave the words a scornful emphasis.

Jilleen grinned at Kris across the table. "I don't mind being reminded once in a while what it's like out there. Oh, yeah, that movie got a little sticky in the end. I mean, when they brought in the hip priest that all the street people followed like a bunch of orphan lambs. I'm an atheist, myself. I don't buy that trip."

Chloe snorted. "Great atheist, you are," she commented dryly. "Last time you landed in Emergency bleeding your life away, the first thing you said when you woke up was, 'Thank God!' "

Jilleen's white skin flushed a radiant pink, but she managed a crooked smile. "Some days I'm not as smart as other days," she said softly. "That's why I'm still underfoot around here, Chloe. Maybe I don't have it all together yet, but I'm working on it."

Chloe nodded. "You'll get there. I wish all you kids would wake up and smell the coffee.

135

You're young, and that's a fine thing to be. To enjoy." Her voice warmed the word.

Easy for you to say, Kris thought.

Her face must have mirrored the silent protest, because Chloe looked at her quizzically. "All of you came from homes where you couldn't be happy, for one reason or another," she said, her voice quiet. "This is a halfway place. You're safe here, and you have the things you need, even if they aren't very fancy. Somebody's always close by to help you get your head straight, someone who wants to see you make it."

She turned to Jilleen. "That's all the priest in the movie was doing, letting those kids know that somebody cared about them."

Jilleen shrugged. "I suppose. Being alone — really alone — that's the pits, for sure."

Kris remained at the table after Frog and Jilleen rinsed their dishes and departed. She said to Chloe tentatively, "I've been wondering about something. About — clothes."

The woman's expression changed subtly, as if she had expected to hear something else. Then she nodded, lips pursed. "You're here on a temporary basis, but I could look into a clothing allowance."

"No," Kris said. She shook her head. "No, it was my own dumb fault that I lost my things. I'd rather go out and earn some money on my own."

"Good idea." Chloe smiled. "And I'm glad it

136

came from you. I have a tough time with some of my kids, because they don't want to take the consequences of their own actions." She added irrelevantly, "That's a nice boyfriend you have."

"He liked you, too." Kris smiled at her. "Then it's all right if I find a job washing windows or baby-sitting, something like that?"

"Sure." Chloe thought for a moment. "Why don't you go down to the Youth Center? Seems to me they have a list of summer jobs for kids."

"There isn't any rule for kids from out of town?" Kris asked. "You don't have to pay a registration fee?" On impulse, she told Chloe about her experience at the employment agency.

The brown eyes narrowed. "Dirty crook!" she said angrily. "Ripping off kids. She ought to be reported."

"No," Kris said once more, "I don't think she'll try it again. And I chalked it up to experience. That was a rotten day, all right. So what you said just now about being young and enjoying it — well, I was thinking how rough it can be. Every time you turn around, people like that hassling you. There was a lady who had me wash all her windows and — " She told Chloe about that, too.

Then she paused, deciding she had said enough. She was surprised, in fact, at all she had told Chloe. "Well, I guess I'll get started. Is the Youth Center nearby?"

Chloe gave her directions. "Would you like to take a sack lunch? Good. You go get ready, and I'll fix it."

It turned out to be a lucky day. Kris found a job a few blocks from the Center, cleaning kitchen cupboards for a harried mother with three small children. She helped feed the little ones and put them down for naps before she finished her work.

"You're absolutely wonderful with kids," the young woman told her with a sigh. "Any chance I could hire you for a couple mornings a week?"

"Oh, yes, that'd be great."

Kris went home, tired and eager for a shower, but excited and happy about the money she had earned. She would have a new blouse and sandals to wear to the zoo when Regan picked her up Friday morning.

Pink, she thought. She'd look for a pink blouse. This time when Mindy's face popped up in her mind, it didn't hurt quite as much as it once had.

It seemed natural, too, to share the story of her day with Jilleen. Refreshed by her shower and comfortably cool in shorts, she found the red-headed girl in the kitchen making a pitcher of iced tea.

"Did you have any luck?" Jilleen handed her a tall frosty glass.

"Mmm, that's what I need. It was so hot today, I'm practically dehydrated." Kris drank thirstily, then sat at the table to describe her new job.

"I can get a new outfit to wear on Friday." She made a small contented sound. "A pink blouse, I think."

Jilleen nodded. "Pink would be fantastic. With your skin and coloring — " She saw Kris wince. "Did I say something wrong?"

"No, it's just that — " Before she realized it, she had poured out the story of Mindy's betrayal.

"So she took off with the blouse and everything else." Jilleen's mouth twisted. "And you made up your mind never to let anybody else get close to you."

Kris glanced at her uneasily.

"Join the club. Good thing for you that guy Regan's around, you know that?" She looped her thumbs beneath her long heavy red hair and held it off her neck for a moment. "It really helps when you have one person you can trust. I was here for a whole month before I'd come out of my room, except to go to the bathroom or for meals. Isn't that wild?"

She laughed. "Chloe can tell you the first thing I said to her when I got here. She took me back to the room and I turned and yelled at her, 'You don't like me!' She just grinned and said, 'For heaven's sake, girl, give me five minutes to make up my mind. How do I know whether I like you or not?' "

Kris thought, amused, that sounded like Chloe.

"My problem right then was that I didn't care a whole lot about me, either. I'd been with a lot of guys, passed around like — like a joint or a can of beer, maybe. Nobody put any value on me, so I guess you know the kind of price tag I hung on myself." The gray eyes briefly reflected the pain in those memories.

"Crazy," she said, her voice quiet but without bitterness. "None of those turkeys cared about what *I* wanted, what was important to me. Maybe that's why I wouldn't let myself believe Chloe was for real.

"I've been in foster homes before, you know. One place I never got enough to eat. Oh, the food was on the table, but the lady either burned it or put too much salt in it or something like curry powder that made me sick."

She sipped her tea and went on after a moment. "Or I'd land somewhere and find somebody hitting the booze as bad as my old lady. One time the family had a funny uncle I had to stay clear of. And Frog can tell you about places he's been. The kind where they gave their own kids these great toys and lots of clothes, and he got the beat-up stuff, the hand-me-downs. Listen, this place is really cool."

She looked at Kris. "And Chloe is some kind of lady. She is, you know. So don't be a dummy like I was, hiding in a corner, keeping everybody at arm's length. Believe me, if you're on the same trip I was, trying not to *feel* anything anymore, sooner or later you'll add it up the way I did. You'll figure you might as well be dead."

Kris felt tension humming between them as if they were both holding their breath.

"I talked to Alan the other day," she said at last. "That's about what he said, too. You must think I'm really weird, feeling so sorry for myself. And with all the rotten things that happened to you — God!" She heard horror in her voice and flushed uncomfortably.

Jilleen leaned forward, arms on the table, and Kris found herself staring at the scars on her thin wrists. She seemed unable to look away from the mute evidence of someone else's agony, agony reflected in the stark ugly pictures in her mind.

Though the red-headed girl's voice was soft and casual, her eyes were intent on Kris's face. "You care about what happened to me?"

"Care?" Kris repeated. She said then, almost angrily, "Of course I care."

"Yes, I think you do. So why get so uptight at the idea that people around here might care about you?"

Kris stared at her. "I guess — I was afraid to believe it," she said in a near whisper. "I never thought about it that way."

Jilleen laughed. "Start thinking about it then, just like that."

141

The words lingered in Kris's mind all through dinner.

Dunny inquired about her new job, teasing her, amusement in his eyes. "All these years you've been cleaning house and taking care of kids, and here's somebody paying you good money for it. What do you know about that!"

"I know one thing," she said. "I don't mind doing the dirtiest job there is if somebody appreciates it. That lady paid me, but she kept thanking me over and over, too. I felt just as good about that as I did about the money."

He blinked, and she suspected he was a little startled by the longest speech he had heard from her yet.

"Good point," he said. "I try to remember that, myself, when somebody does a job for me. Fellow down at the garage told me once, there's only about half a dozen of his regular customers who bother thanking him. Then he winked and said he'd let me guess who gets priority on his time."

Frog's head came up abruptly. Kris had noted that the boy hung on every word Dunny said.

"I used to work my butt off for my old man," he said in his harsh voice. "Only time he paid attention was when I didn't do it good enough or quick enough. Then I really caught it."

Dunny grunted. "Well, he was too far one way when it came to punishing," he agreed.

"Some parents can't bring themselves to punish at all or set any limits. That can be wrong, too. Somebody's going to be the boss in the house, the father or mother — or the kid. You go along with that?"

After a moment, Frog nodded. Kris watched, intrigued by the shift in the conversation.

"Okay, Frog, some day you'll have kids of your own. What kind of father are you going to be? Say your kid is five or six years old, and he does something bad. You really have to make a point. How would you handle it?"

Light glittered in the round glasses as the boy tipped back his head, thinking about it.

"I'd give him a swat, I guess. But then I'd hug him and tell him I loved him. I'd want him to grow up good, that's all."

Dunny chuckled. "If you told him that, too, I'd say you'd make the point, all right."

Kris sat deep in thought long after the others had left the table. Once the dishwasher hummed into action, Chloe turned to her, wiping her hands on a kitchen towel.

"Would you like another glass of iced tea?"

"What? Oh — yes, thanks."

The pet door flapped, and Joe ambled in from the back porch.

Kris stiffened as he paused to look at her with his sad brown eyes.

"Joe, you old beggar," Chloe laughed. "Well, I guess a couple of dog biscuits won't ruin you."

She reached into the cupboard and tossed them on the table. "Kris, want to take your turn spoiling him?"

"I — " The refusal stuck in her throat. She stared at the biscuits, her face hot.

"I'm sorry, honey. I never thought to ask you if you like dogs. Come to think of it, you haven't warmed up much to Joe."

Chloe sat down with a soft groan. "I'm not a cat person, myself. Can't abide them. But my sister Neva couldn't get along without her old calico. To each his own, I reckon."

"It's not — it's not that." Kris took a deep breath to still the trembling inside. "I had a dog once. Jebber. He — oh, damn, I didn't want to cry! He — Joe looks just — just like him. It's like he's — it's like looking at a g-ghost!"

She found herself sobbing into the towel thrust into her hands. At last, the tears subsiding, she gave Chloe a watery smile.

Chloe nodded and said with satisfaction, "I *knew* you were a dog person. Anybody as smart as you are — though the good Lord knows you haven't begun to use half the brains He gave you."

Kris gave a shaky laugh. "That's crazy," she said. "Now, that's just plain crazy. What do brains have to do with it? You don't love dogs with your brains."

"No, love comes from the heart. Funny thing, though. Who would you say were the

144

happiest people you know, the kind that are all heart or all brain?"

Kris grinned, but she answered the question with another. "Wouldn't people be happier if they were half and half?"

"Ah!" Chloe looked pleased. "Smart, that's what you are. Now, when you get around to working it that way, using everything you've got, why you'll just naturally be a whole lot happier for it."

Kris had to laugh at Chloe's obvious delight at the success of her little trap. She looked down to see Joe's head a few inches from her knee as he waited politely for the biscuits on the table.

He responded to her glance with a soft whine, chin raised, tail whipping the air in a small frenzy. Like Jeb's tail, it resembled a piece of raveled rope. When she handed him the biscuits, he settled at her feet to crunch them noisily.

"You win," Kris said and couldn't be sure whether she spoke to Chloe or the old dog.

Chapter
Twelve

"I was looking at the calendar today," Regan said. "It's been three weeks since you moved in with Chloe. So what do you think? About next fall, I mean."

They were lying on the sun-warmed grass in Presidio Park. A wide expanse of lawn sloped gently to the parking area below. For a while, after wandering through the museum, they sat and talked, watching three little kids roll down the slope and climb, breathless with laughter, to roll down again.

After a few minutes, Kris looked at Regan and grinned, and they got up to try it themselves. Now they rested, tired and happy, content with the day and each other.

Until Regan's vaguely troubled question.

"What do I think?" Kris repeated. She chewed reflectively on a blade of grass. Alan had asked the question, too, a few days ago. And Chloe had spoken about school only yesterday, inquiring about the classes Kris planned to take. Everyone seemed to be nudging her toward some decision, one she still felt unwilling to make.

"You mean, do I want to stay here and go to school?"

Regan glanced at her. "What I really mean is, have you thought how great it would be if we could go back to school together?"

Kris felt her face stiffen. "I don't think — anything's changed — back home."

"There's a chance you're wrong about that. But that isn't what I said." He rolled onto his back and squinted up at the sky. "It's been really fantastic, calling you on the phone whenever I want, seeing you so often."

She said after a moment, "Long Beach isn't that far."

"Too far to see you as often as I'd want to. I'm carrying a heavy load next year, and I'll be working part-time. This is my last goof-off summer with college coming up."

Kris was silent. One part of her mind accepted the truth in what he said. But the other part rejected it, a little hurt because he had been so blunt. If he really cared about her, he wouldn't consider for one minute any possibility that she'd want to go back to everything she had run away from.

"Kris?"

She looked at him, trying to smile.

"Don't do that," he said, touching her face. "Don't go back in your shell. The way we feel about each other, we should be able to talk. About anything at all."

"I thought we could," she said. "But you don't seem to understand. After everything I've told you, don't you see it would never work?"

"Not the way it was before, no. But it might be different."

"My mother won't ever change."

"People do." His voice was quiet, urgent. "You've changed, Kris."

"She won't."

"How can you be so sure? Have you written to her? Talked to her?"

She turned away. "You know I haven't."

A short silence.

She sat up then, scowling down at him. "You don't know her, Regan. I do. She hasn't called me or written me, either, has she?"

He lay quietly, hands behind his head, smiling up at her. But he said nothing.

Exasperated, she blurted, "Okay! If I do call her and she's — she's just like always — will you stop hassling me about it?"

"Yup."

She swallowed hard, already regretting her hasty words. Her stomach churned as she thought about talking to her mother, hearing that sharp impatient voice again, cold with anger.

"Want me to be there?" Regan sat up and grabbed her hand. "I'll put the call through if you want. And afterwards, I'll take you to Farrell's for a sundae, double fudge."

She tried to pull away, but he held her, both hands around hers.

"You — !" she said. "O'Flannery Regan, you — !"

"That did it." He released her hand so suddenly, she fell sideways on the grass. He grinned. "We oughta fight more often. You really give off sparks when you're mad enough to knock my head off."

She stared at him. "Is it that important to you, Regan, to make us come close to — to a real fight?"

His smile faded. "Not to me," he said. "I think this might be important to you. You can't write off sixteen years of living with someone — and go on as if it never happened. You're just not the kind of girl who can do that."

"I can try," she said.

Regan cuffed her gently. "You've been trying for three weeks, and it's still making you sick inside every time you think about it. Don't you think I know that? Every time I mention Long Beach, your face gets all tight, and you change the subject."

He added with emphasis, "Settle it, Kris, once and for all. Say what you want to say to your mother and hear her out, too. Then you'll know where you stand."

By the time she got home, she admitted to herself that he was probably right about that. When you closed a door for good, maybe you should take one last look at what was behind it, to make sure you were doing the wise thing. Even though she was sure she had acted in the only way possible, it might help to reassure herself about that. Maybe that would heal the place inside that still hurt each time her thoughts touched upon it.

Unluckily, this was the night her mother worked late. She would have to wait till morning to call. Now her thoughts returned again and again, compulsively, to explore an area of wincing pain.

She found the household in a state of tension. Closing the front door behind her, she stopped to listen to strange sounds from Frog's bedroom. When she crossed the living room, she saw a sign tacked to his door.

The message read in straggling black letters, "All you rats stay out of here!"

Jilleen called to her from the kitchen and explained with a scornful gleam in her gray eyes, "Frog's declared war. He's lying on his bed in there, kicking the wall."

"Barefoot," Chloe said, turning from the stove. "He's kicking it with his bare feet."

"So give him points for that."

"What happened?" Kris sat at the table and smiled down at Joe who promptly moved closer, propping his chin on her knees so she could scratch behind his ears.

"He left the lawnmower out overnight. All the tools, in fact. He's been restricted, so now he's trying to punish us, too." Jilleen sounded disgusted.

Kris glanced at her, puzzled by the sharpness in her voice.

"He's fourteen years old," Chloe said mildly.

"Well, it's time he shaped up. He acts like he's about four, sometimes."

"He still has things to work out. Let him do it his way. He's only testing, you know that, pushing against the guidelines to see if they'll hold."

Jilleen tossed her hair back with unnecessary violence. "Listen, that little son-of-a — " She broke off, glancing at Chloe, and vivid color came into her face. She sounded even angrier when she went on.

"He's been here longer than any of us. He knows good and well nobody's going to change the rules on his account. He's a pain with all his *testing*."

Chloe stirred the contents of the pan, and the rich, warm smell of onions and tomato sauce drifted through the kitchen.

"Jilleen," she said, "if you make too many demands on people, you'll go through life disappointed. The way I see it, life's too short to waste it being mad all the time because people around you don't measure up."

She shook her head, listening to another furious tattoo from Frog's room. "He'll have his heels worn down to the anklebone," she muttered.

"I'd like to wear down his *head* bone for him. With a two-by-four." Jilleen whirled and left the room, yelling at Frog as she passed his door, "Shut up in there! Will you just knock off the racket!"

There was a muffled reply from Frog before he resumed the rhythmic pounding.

Chloe didn't look up. She addressed the spoon in her short stubby fingers as if continuing a shared dialog. "Seems to me, there's more than one kid around this house pushing against the guidelines. Always shoving against them to see if maybe, just once, they'll move back a little."

She sighed. "And what a big disappointment that would be. If something in life didn't hold firm and solid and dependable."

"Chloe?"

The little woman turned, her brown eyes startled, as if she had forgotten she wasn't alone.

"You're unreal," Kris said softly. "Doesn't it ever get to you? Dozens of kids you take in, and all of us floundering around trying to get ourselves together, hassling you, yelling our heads off," — she laughed as she heard Frog renew his assault on the wall — "kicking the wall — "

"Barefoot," Chloe pointed out once more with a chuckle. "He always takes his shoes off." She studied Kris for a moment. "Frog can go just so long before he flies off the handle and turns his back on all of us. But when I remember what's on that back, well, I don't need a degree in psychology to understand what's going on inside him."

She stared at the spoon, her eyes intent. "And I'm not any saint just because I have a little extra patience when he acts like this. I recall too well how he was when he came, never a peep out of him, creeping around the house like a sick pup."

She paused to listen for a few seconds and give Kris a crooked smile. "Nothing like a little yelling and hollering and banging on the wall to let off steam. Won't hurt the wall a bit, and nothing's bottled up to get his insides all riled."

Corrosive emotions, Alan had called it, Kris thought. She remembered another day when he had clutched his head in mock despair as they discussed Chloe.

"I have a couple of degrees, two years of work in the field," he said. "And I can't honestly say I do anything better than she does.

153

That lady goes by pure instinct — and a lot of common sense. I wish we had a dozen just like her."

For several minutes, Kris sat deep in thought, wondering about Jilleen's over-reaction to Frog's tantrum. Chloe had suggested that she made too many demands on people, only to be disappointed when they failed to measure up.

The old testing game. Funny how Jilleen could see Frog playing that game, unaware that she did it, herself. Did everyone try to take a turn making the rules? *Do I?* Kris thought. Did she send silent signals to other people?

If you really care about me, you'll behave the way I want you to . . .

She thought back to the afternoon, the way she had felt when Regan kept chipping away at the idea that she might go back home. Yes, she must have the same blind spot. Even though she had agreed to call her mother, accepting with reluctance the fact that he might be right about that, she had been cross with him, even hurt.

Admit it, she told herself. She had been disappointed in him. How could he suggest such a thing if he truly cared about her? That's what she had thought.

She looked up to find Chloe watching her.

Amusement sparkled in the lively brown eyes. "Did I say something to you?" the little woman inquired. "Or was it Frog or Jilleen talking to you?"

"All of you, I guess." Kris took a deep breath. "And Alan and Regan. It seems as if all of a sudden, I'm listening. You know? I remember how I felt back home — "

For a moment, she recalled the old frustration and anger so strongly, she could almost taste the bitterness in her mouth.

"Because nobody ever listened to me," she said slowly. "I thought for a while that Mindy did, but for some reason, she liked stirring me up. I still don't know why. She always had a reason, though, for everything she did. There was always something in it for Mindy."

Chloe said after a short silence, "You'll know a Mindy next time you bump into one. Too bad we have to learn that way, getting our lumps along with the lessons. Important thing is, can you look back now without letting it tear you up all over again?"

"Yes," Kris said. "Lately I can. You know, I used to wonder about Mindy sometimes. I mean, I'd get so mad at my family, it made me sick. I'd actually throw up, or I'd have trouble getting to sleep at night.

"The thing is, she had a really rotten time of it at home, too. Her mother was drunk all the time. And they'd fight — all three of them when her father was home. But it never *bothered* her."

"Happens that way once in a while." Chloe shook her head. "When things get so bad in a family, everybody stops caring. You can only hurt so much before you back away from whatever it is that's making you hurt — or whoever it is that's doing it."

Kris stared at her. "She used to say she didn't care." In her mind, she heard Mindy's careless words: "I don't care about either of them, and they don't care about me. Simple as that."

"I didn't believe her," she said in a low voice. "Isn't that crazy? All the time, she meant just what she said."

"The poor sad, sorry child." Chloe's voice mourned for all sad, sorry children. "She'll find out some day when you turn off the caring part of yourself, it isn't that easy to turn it on again."

"For sure," Kris muttered.

"Good thing for you, you never turned it off." Chloe moved the pan to the back of the stove and lifted her apron to wipe her flushed face.

Kris shifted in her chair uneasily. After a moment, she said, "Maybe I care about the people here, Chloe. About you — and Alan — and Regan. But — "

Chloe laughed. "But you've stopped caring about those people back in Long Beach? Honey, I swear you've only been listening with one ear, and that one stuffed full of cotton.

"The day you stop caring, that'll be the day you don't feel like there's a flock of hornets fighting inside you every time you think about home. About your mother and that sister, Patsy, and those little brothers of yours."

She added, her voice firm, "You hurt when you think about them, don't you? Then mark my words, child, as sure as Joe's scratching right now where a flea just bit him, you still *care*."

Chapter
Thirteen

Kris felt her stomach jumping with nerves as she held the phone and listened to the muted ringing on the line. She hoped Patsy would answer. Then she could go and tell her mother it was Kris calling, give her a little warning.

What if her mother didn't want to talk to her?

That would settle it, wouldn't it? For once and for all, it would be settled, over and done with. For a moment it hurt to breathe. Why didn't somebody answer?

At last she heard someone lift the receiver, cutting off the buzz on the line. Her mother's voice, low-pitched, brusque. "Hello?"

Mouth dry, Kris stammered, "Mother?"

"Kris! Kris, is that you?"

She could detect surprise in the voice, nothing more. "Yes, it's me. I thought I'd call and — and talk to you."

She had planned exactly what to say. She hadn't been able to get to sleep last night because she kept going over the speech in her mind again and again. All for nothing. It went out of her head the moment she heard her mother's voice. She couldn't recall a word she had memorized so carefully.

"Well, I'm glad," her mother said. "I'm glad you called. It's good to hear from you."

Kris thought, startled, her mother sounded nervous, too, as tense and uncertain as she was. "How are things at home? I mean, how are you all?"

"Pretty well. We're about the same, I guess. How are you, Kris? Are you — are you happy?"

She couldn't recall that anyone had ever asked her that question. The last person in the world she had expected to show any interest in her well-being was her mother. She never had before.

As long as Kris could remember, her mother had been too busy, too tired, too tied up in her own problems to think much about her oldest daughter, let alone care about her, care whether or not she was happy.

"Yes," she said and went on quickly, the words tumbling over each other now, because

159

she couldn't bear to have her mother say any more just then. It would make her cry if she did. It might even make her hope again, and she remembered too well the pain and frustration in hope forever unfulfilled.

"It's a very nice place here," she said. "Chloe and Dunny are really great, and there are two other kids. Frog's fourteen and Jilleen's seventeen. And we get along fine. I have a job, too, helping a lady who has three little kids. I work two mornings a week, so I'm earning money."

She stopped to catch her breath.

A short silence. Then, "I'd like to see you, Kris. If you don't work weekends, would you — would you like to come home to visit? Next weekend, maybe? I'll send you the bus fare."

"No, I have enough money — " Kris bit her lip. She had spoken before she stopped to consider whether or not she really wanted to go home for a visit. With that big mouth of hers, she had committed herself a second time without stopping to think what she really wanted to do.

It rattled her so she couldn't come up with a quick excuse, either. "All right," she said. "I'll be up next Saturday. I'll call you from the bus station."

"Good. Well, this is costing you money. We'll save our visiting until then. Until Saturday. Thank you for calling, Kris."

The line went dead. Kris sat for several minutes, staring at the receiver before she hung up.

Thank you for calling. Unreal, she thought, her mother actually thanking her, especially for something as minor as a phone call.

Had her mother read more into her call than she intended? Did she think Kris had called because she was homesick, that she could talk her into coming home to stay? Back to that rat race? Well, maybe it would be a good idea to go for a visit, to talk face to face. It would be easier that way to get that idea out of her head, if that's what she was thinking.

A visit couldn't do any harm. It would be neat to see the twins again, even old Patsy, and Mrs. Kelly and — and let them all know she was getting along okay, that she was perfectly content to stay where she was.

The week passed all too quickly. Her job took two mornings, and the duty roster at Chloe's had rotated her back to the dusting and vacuuming chores.

She and Regan spent one whole day at the zoo, as well. Regan was obviously pleased by the news that she would be spending the weekend in Long Beach.

She told him about the phone call as they were sitting on a bench watching the bears perform for a bus driver talking over the speaker system.

"Up!" he commanded. "Come on, get up there!" As the great beasts rose awkwardly to sit on their hind legs, he tossed them their reward, a few slices of bread.

161

Kris touched Regan's hand. "Please," she said, "don't get your hopes up for a big hearts-and-flowers family reunion. I sort of got roped into it before I realized what was happening." She smiled wryly. "Like I got roped into making the call, in the first place."

He grinned. "Are you sorry now? That you called her, I mean?"

She said thoughtfully, "No, not really. It might be a good thing for both of us. We can talk, I think. I was surprised at the way she — well, it was different than before, I'll say that much."

"Different? How?"

"She sounded as if — as if she was glad to hear from me."

He squeezed her hand. "Did that surprise you? Didn't you really think she'd miss you, Kris?"

She gave a short laugh. "I'll tell you the truth. I didn't think she'd miss anything but — somebody to do the work around the house, someone to watch the kids. And I figured she'd be really steamed because I walked out on her. I let her down. That's the way her mind works."

She turned to look at him. "You've got a nice family, Regan. Your aunt and uncle are great. So it's probably hard for you to get the picture. But there are people like us, like my mother and all of us kids. We lived together, sure, but we never felt or acted like a real family."

He nodded. "Well, you know I used to go around pretty good with my old man, too. I have a hunch he's a lot like your mother. It isn't easy for him to show what he feels unless he's ticked off about something. My mother sort of acted like a buffer, telling me how my dad felt about things, what kind of person he was. I guess she did the same thing with him. It's been cool for about a year now, no big blow-ups about anything."

He added after a moment, "If every family had somebody like my mother or Chloe — "

"Don't look at *me!*" Kris shook her head. "In our case, it would have to be me telling the other kids what Mom's really like. Well, I haven't been able to figure her out, myself. Anyway, I'm not planning to go back to stay. I just want to make sure she's not planning on it, either."

"You're going to visit," he said, sounding happy about that. "You can see all of them. You'll feel better once you've had a chance to talk."

Kris couldn't be as sure about that as he obviously was. But then, Regan didn't know her family, she thought. How could he possibly know what she was feeling? How could he even guess at the apprehension she felt? It grew with every passing day, a cold buzzing vacuum in her stomach.

On Friday, she bought new tennies and a yellow blouse to wear with her denims. That night, she packed everything in the straw bag, tucking in a big bag of oranges that Chloe picked from the tree in the backyard.

"Nervous?" Chloe asked the next morning on the way to the bus station. She laughed as she glanced at Kris's hands, tightly clenched in her lap. "Honey, I'd be willing to bet you aren't half as nervous as your mother is right this minute. I can hear her yelling at those kids to hop to it and clean up the kitchen, get the house picked up while she's busy cooking — what is it you liked best that she used to cook on days she was off work?"

"Chicken and dumplings, I guess," Kris said after a moment's thought. "I never could get the hang of dumplings. They always came out soggy and doughy or rubbery. And once every five years or so, she made a chocolate cake, the kind you make with mayonnaise. Heavenly!"

She laughed. "I'm willing to bet you're wrong, though. Like I told Regan the other day, you just don't know my mother. She'll probably fix hamburgers or meatloaf. Why make a big thing over me coming for a visit? I'm the rotten kid who ran away, remember?"

Chloe snorted. "You're no rotten kid, Kris, and you know it. You're smart and you're honest and people can depend on you. If they treat you fair and square, they can. It triggers your temper when people rip you off."

She paused to smile. "That's a real good way

you young ones put it when somebody does you wrong."

A satisfied jerk of her head. "You're smarter than lots of kids your age, I'd say. I think you've got a good idea of the ways you're strong and the things you still have to learn. Physically, you're mature. Emotionally, not yet. But you'll get there. Look at the way you cotton to that boy of yours, Regan. And he to you."

Kris sighed. "Sometimes I wonder what he sees in me. I'm so mixed up, I sure can't see much of anything wonderful."

Chloe chuckled. "He sees what everybody else sees in you, honey. You've got *style*, girl, don't you know that?"

Kris burst out laughing, both startled and amused. If Chloe insisted she was pretty or that she had a terrific personality, she would have shrugged off the remark, certain by this time of just one thing. Chloe truly cared about her.

But *style*? During the ride to Long Beach, she returned again and again to the word and the moment in which it had been spoken. She remembered commenting once a little sadly about her lost possessions, not only her clothes but the little Hummel figurine and the charm bracelet Mrs. Kelly had given her.

Chloe had told her, "All you'll ever have that you can count on keeping is what you are."

What am I? Kris thought now. *I'm not really sure. But Chloe says I have style.* She treasured the words, knew she would find comfort in them during moments when she felt low. They would be something to live up to, as well. Chloe had a way of making you stretch a little and in so doing, you sometimes achieved more than you thought you could.

She called her mother from the bus depot, glad she would have a few minutes to brace herself for the meeting. It might be only a little more than a month since she left home, but it seemed much longer.

"We're the same, I guess," her mother had said. Well, of course they would be the same. Nothing would have changed at home. But she had. She must make sure they all understood how much she had changed.

When her mother came through the big glass doors at last, Kris had a bad moment. She felt her legs shaking as she went to meet her, her smile tremulous. They exchanged only a casual greeting.

"Hi."

"You got here, I see. I had to park up in the next block."

"Man, it's hot. I'm glad I brought my shorts."

"That's a pretty outfit. Yellow's good on you. I don't remember you ever had anything in that shade before. I can't wear it, myself. My skin's too sallow."

She looked the same, Kris thought, trying to relax. Her white pantsuit was an old one. The streets of Long Beach were unchanged. The only difference she detected now was the constraint between her and her mother, clearly revealed in the awkward polite comments they exchanged, the meaningless small talk of strangers.

The minute the car pulled into the drive, she saw the door to the house fly open. Patsy and the twins came tumbling out to greet her. Kris had a hard time controlling a shaky smile when the twins took turns hugging her so hard, her ribs ached.

"Are you gonna stay?" Greg demanded. "Boy, we really missed you."

"We missed your cooking, that's for sure. You wouldn't believe what we got to eat while you were gone." Guy made a gagging sound, clutching his throat with both hands. "Old Patsy burns everything."

"Always griping," Patsy told him angrily. "World's biggest griper, that's what you are." She grinned at Kris, her face flushing. "That's a really neat blouse."

Why, she feels shy with me, Kris thought, surprised. Patsy's skin looked a little better. She hadn't lost any weight, but her hair had been cut and she must have just washed it.

Kris hugged her. "Hey, your hair looks great."

Her mother made shooing motions at them. "For heaven's sake, let her go in the house,

167

will you? All the fuss you're making, you'd think she'd been gone for years. You boys! Take her bag back to her room."

The twins argued loudly over possession of the straw bag. At last they each took one of the handles and carried it between them.

Patsy followed the small caravan into the back bedroom, apparently noting Kris's surprise that it looked exactly the same, even to her clothes and shoes in the closet.

"Yeah," Patsy said on a note of chagrin. "Mom said she'd skin me if she caught me wearing anything of yours." After a moment she added, "She did, too."

Kris had to laugh. "Well, it'll help. I lost nearly everything I took with me."

"Lost it?" Patsy sat on the bed and looked at her curiously. "What happened? How could you lose all your clothes?"

From the door, her mother said crossly, "Didn't I tell you not to go asking a lot of questions? It's not any of your affair what happened to Kris *or* her things. And I don't want to have to tell you again, do you understand?"

"Okay, okay."

"Good. Everybody get washed up for lunch. We can talk at the table."

Kris took her time in the bathroom. It had never occurred to her that her mother would have guarded so fiercely the possessions she had left behind. Why? Had she been so sure that Kris would come home again? Was she still certain of it? Perhaps, the unexpected warmth of this homecoming had been carefully calculated to persuade her daughter.

Over sandwiches and some of Chloe's oranges, the twins dominated the conversation. Laughing, interrupting each other, they boasted about how well they could ride the birthday bicycle.

Mrs. Kelly popped in for coffee and cookies, hugging Kris and exclaiming happily over her beautiful tan set off by the new blouse.

Kris felt a little more comfortable with the neighbor present to prevent any more pointed questions. She talked easily about Chloe and Dunny, about Frog and Jilleen, and the home they shared.

"Hey!" Guy blurted abruptly. "Do they have a dog?"

"Guy," his mother said, eyeing him until he squirmed.

"I just wondered," he protested. "I only thought how much she likes dogs."

"Matter of fact," Kris said, "we do have a dog. His name is Joe." She went on to explain why Chloe had given him the name. But when she tried to tell them how much he looked like Jeb, the words stuck in her throat. She couldn't talk about Jeb in the place still haunted by his ghost.

It was a surprisingly pleasant day, unmarred

by the recriminations she had half expected, almost free of quarrels except for a few minor squabbles between Patsy and the twins.

Her mother actually fixed chicken and dumplings for dinner that night, and when she discovered there would be a chocolate "mayonnaise cake" for dessert, Kris laughed out loud. Then she had to tell her mother that Chloe had predicted the menu that morning.

"Well, she was a good prophet." Mrs. Wilding smiled, looking pleased. "She — Chloe sounds like a nice person. I'm glad she's been good to you, Kris."

As she drifted off to sleep that night, her bed feeling comfortably familiar, Kris felt a little troubled, nevertheless. Her mother had made no attempt to talk to her privately, to question her or to discuss the future.

Perhaps that was just as well, Kris decided. That talk might well be unpleasant for both of them. At least they had kept from spoiling the first day of her visit. It would be wise, no doubt, to delay the conversation until her last hours in the house in Long Beach.

Chapter
Fourteen

Her mother must have dreaded the prospect of a serious talk between them as much as Kris did. In any event, it was late the next afternoon before she broached the subject.

Patsy and Kris were back in the bedroom discussing Patsy's new and eager interest in dieting. Too casually, she mentioned a new boy on the street, and Kris suspected he had a lot to do with her sister's sudden desire for a new image.

She looked up to see her mother at the door.

"Kris, why don't you come out to the kitchen now?" Mrs. Wilding suggested. "I'd like to talk to you about your — your plans." She glanced at Patsy. "I want you to stay back here while we're talking."

Kris noted the disappointment on Patsy's face. "I'd like her to sit in," she said to her mother and saw a flicker of irritation in the dark eyes so like her own. "Any plans we're talking about, well, they'll involve Patsy, too, you know. We're a family."

In the echo of the words, she thought sadly, they were not yet a family in the most important meaning of the word. All of them had a lot to learn about living together.

"All right," her mother said and turned to precede them down the hall.

Patsy bounced to her feet with a wide grin. "Hey, thanks!" she whispered. In the kitchen, she perched on the edge of her chair, her eyes sparkling. She even accepted a cup of tea.

Kris suppressed a smile, knowing how her sister detested the beverage. For once, Patsy would be in on a family discussion, she thought, a part of the planning process. This time, she wouldn't have to listen at keyholes or crouched around a corner in the hall.

At last her mother settled at the table with a sigh. A frown creased her forehead and drew her mouth into a tight severe line.

Kris sipped her tea, aware of the flutters in her stomach, trying to ignore them. "Patsy and I have been talking," she said. "It sounds like she's really trying hard to do a good job around here."

Her mother made a sharp gesture. "She's trying, I guess. I don't expect a lot from her."

Patsy's face tightened as if she'd been slapped. She opened her mouth, but Kris touched her hand before she could erupt in angry protest.

To her mother, Kris said evenly, "You sure expected a lot from me." The words hung in the air between them for a long moment.

"If I asked a lot of you, it was because I could trust you," her mother said, her voice edged with impatience. "You were the responsible one, the one with a head on your shoulders. Didn't you understand that?"

"How could I when you never told me?"

"I'm telling you now." One thin hand brushed her eyes and mouth. "I figured you were the one who'd get through college, make something of yourself."

She looked at Patsy then. "You wanted to sit in on this. Okay, then listen good. You're too lazy, too flighty. It's hard to tell how you'll turn out. Only thing I've ever been sure of is, I just can't depend on you."

Again, Kris shook her head at her sister. And once more Patsy subsided, looking a little startled by this new development, a sister who wanted to speak in her behalf, who might even stick up for her.

"I don't remember that you ever tried to depend on her," Kris said, her voice soft. "You never gave her any responsibility. She got away with murder. You put me square in the middle. Well, that wasn't good for any of us."

Patsy jerked her hand away, looking betrayed.

"Listen," Kris said to her urgently. "It's time to be honest about everything that's happened. And that means we all get a chance to talk, to say how we feel. Okay?"

"I guess so," Patsy said reluctantly, "if I get a chance, too."

"You will. That's why I wanted you to sit in." Kris turned back to her mother. "It hasn't been easy for you since Dad left, we know that. But I don't think you realize that it hasn't been that great for any of us, either."

"Of course I realize that!" Her mother flushed angrily. "Could I help it if your dad ran off, never gave us any money? There's never been enough money. Don't you think I wanted things to be easier for you?"

"You've worked really hard," Kris agreed, "at a job you've always hated. All of us appreciate that. We know that money's been a problem."

"Well, then?"

"What I'm trying to tell you is, we've tried to see your problems, but you never seemed to care about what went on here at home. You put me in charge, right?"

"You were the oldest. The dependable one," her mother said. The words were underlined with bitterness. "Seems I was wrong about that."

Kris felt a wave of anger rise to choke back her words for a moment. She felt the hot blood burning in her cheeks when she retorted at last, "I did the best I could. You never thanked me, never praised me for anything I did. But what made it even worse, you never listened to me when I tried to tell you what went on. As long as you could pull my chain, you never cared whether Patsy and the twins helped me or not. You didn't care how I felt about it."

Her voice was harsh now with the strain that tightened her throat. "When I talked to you on the phone Friday, I couldn't believe it when you thanked me for calling, when you asked if I was happy."

"I'm your mother. Why wouldn't I care whether you were okay, how you were feeling? Even though you didn't give much thought to me when you took off the way you did."

Her mother stirred her tea, her hand trembling. "You'll never know what I went through those three days before I heard — that you were all right. Alive. Not — not — " Her lips pressed together in a straight thin line.

"I'm sorry," Kris said slowly. "Whether you believe it or not, it simply never occurred to me that you'd care a whole lot. You never said you did, and you sure never showed it. How was I supposed to know?"

Her mother said nothing, staring now at the spoon beside her cup.

"Patsy?" Kris looked at her sister. "What would you like to say?"

Her sister stared at her. After a moment, she sighed loudly. "I guess you said it better than I can. It's been awful around here, lots worse than when you were home. You seemed to manage a lot better."

Tears filled her eyes and spilled over. "All the cooking and the laundry and trying to keep the house clean — and the boys won't help. They just l-laugh at me, and I'm yelling at them all the time and — and nobody *cares* how I feel!"

Her mother's head came up, her eyes narrowed. "That's just what I thought would happen if you sat in on this. The two of you would gang up on me. All I'd hear is just what you've both been saying, what a lousy mother I am, how put-upon you are!"

She turned to Kris, furious now, her own eyes full of tears. "I suppose you thought you'd come home and whip us all in line just by telling us how Chloe runs *her* house. A list of rules and a poster on your bedroom wall and jobs on the bulletin board. Everybody getting along, all sweetness and light. You were going to move back in and show us how *easy* it is!"

Kris shook her head wearily. Once again, she had failed to communicate, and she felt the burden of that failure weigh more heavily than ever before. This time, she had failed Patsy, too.

"No, you're wrong about that," she said. "I didn't mean to make it sound simple. Maybe I have talked too much about Chloe, but I didn't do it to make you feel bad. Really I didn't. And I never wanted you to think that I planned to move back home, either."

Her mother pushed her chair back so quickly, the tea in her cup sloshed into the saucer.

As she left the kitchen, Patsy began to sob. "It could be better," she said miserably. "It could be different. But she won't ever listen. She doesn't care! Oh, Kris if you'd just come back to stay."

"Patsy, I can't. Don't you see? Nothing's changed. I took it as long as I could, until I couldn't take any more. Well, I found out what it's like on the road, worse than you can possibly imagine. I was just lucky, landing at Chloe's." On the verge of tears, herself, she ended in a whisper, "I just can't come back here."

The ugly scene haunted her during the bus ride home that evening. The visit had been a mistake, she thought. Now she felt a new torment, the scratch of guilt because Patsy was stuck now in the same routine that had driven her from home.

What if Patsy decided to run away? She hadn't been able to promise her much in the way of help except that she would write every week and call as often as she could.

On the drive from the bus depot, she told Chloe what had happened. She said at last, hunched in her corner of the car, "It's so rotten for Patsy. She's grown up a lot, I think. I feel like a rat, leaving her in that awful mess."

Chloe clucked. "People can change and do, but hardly ever overnight," she said. "Honey, all I can tell you is, you left your mama with a lot to chew on. When you write, you make those letters to all the family, hear? Nice newsy, cheerful letters — better keep me out of them, though — and we'll see what we'll see."

One week went by, then two. Kris wrote to tell the twins more about Joe, about Frog's new hamster named Herman and how Frog claimed proudly that he was potty-trained. She sent Patsy a diet that looked fairly simple and inexpensive. And she enclosed a meatloaf recipe for her mother, together with a note from the lady she worked for.

During the second week, she received a letter addressed in her mother's small pinched writing. Kris opened it warily. There were only a few lines repeating the theme that had come clearly through everything she said during the session around the kitchen table.

"You don't realize how miserable I've been for all these long years, how hard I've worked, how much I wanted for you kids, how I tried."

Somehow, seeing it in writing, something came through to Kris more strongly. Her mother was desperately uncertain about what a mother should *be*, guilty and unhappy about what had gone before.

There was one hopeful note in the short letter in the last lines. "Maybe there's something in what you said," her mother wrote. "We didn't talk to each other enough. Or listen."

Kris folded the letter and put it away in the chest of drawers. She stood for several minutes staring at herself in the mirror, thoughtfully, until she realized she was searching her face for the ways in which she resembled her mother.

She thought then with wry amusement, if her mother really wanted to learn to listen, Patsy would be there to do the talking. The day that Patsy wrote to say her mother was trying to listen, that would be the day she'd consider going home again.

On the last day of August, she came home from her morning job to find Jilleen and Chloe making sandwiches in the kitchen.

"Yum, those look good. I'm starved." Kris sighed. "But I better get a shower first. When I burped the baby, she spit up all down my back."

A few minutes later, she joined Chloe at the table.

"The kids are eating out back," Chloe said. "Sit down and keep me company." Still, she had little to say.

She seemed so unusually quiet and thoughtful that Kris asked as she finished her sandwich, "Is something wrong?"

"Well, as a matter of fact, something's happened that you should know about." Chloe fished in her apron pocket for a newspaper clipping. "I found this in the morning paper."

Kris noted the Imperial Beach dateline and read the item quickly, then again in growing shock.

"The body of a sixteen-year-old girl, apparently the victim of a beating, was found here yesterday by children playing in a vacant lot. Identification of the victim, a runaway from Long Beach, has been established through a stolen wallet found on the body.

"The owner of the wallet, Laura Piggott, is an Imperial Beach woman, manager of a boarding house frequented by transients. Piggott told police the murdered girl gave her name as Mindy Carter.

"Police are hunting Carter's companion, Clifford Franklin, also from Long Beach. Franklin is described as six feet tall, 160 pounds, in his late teens, with black eyes and long black hair worn in a ponytail. He was last seen driving a blue Chevy van covered with surrealistic designs.

"Arizona police have been notified, as Franklin was reported to be heading for the Phoenix area."

Kris looked up at Chloe to say quietly, "She never made it to Arizona, did she?" A moment later, she added with a shudder of realization, "It could have been — it might have been both of us, both Mindy and me."

Chloe nodded, but she said nothing.

"Poor Mindy." Kris swallowed hard. "You know what's the most horrible thing about it? I mean, even more than you'd think reading in the paper that she was only sixteen and — it was an awful way to die. But there's something else you wouldn't know, unless you knew Mindy."

She paused, then went on in a low voice. "There isn't anybody who'll really care, except for me. And how long will I remember Mindy? How many good things *can* I remember about her? Oh, Chloe, isn't that terrible?"

"Yes," Chloe said. "Sad and terrible." She sat in silence for several minutes. Then, as Kris went down the hall, she called to her, "Honey, I almost forgot. There's a letter for you on the table in the family room."

Kris went to get it, saw Patsy's round childish writing and hoped it would be a letter which would cheer her up a little. The news of Mindy had made her sick to her stomach.

"Guess what?" her sister's letter began, then

announced with much underlining and a generous sprinkling of exclamation points that she had lost three pounds on the new diet.

She had even more startling news, Kris discovered on reading the next paragraph.

"Mom asked me the other day about the poster you told us about, if I remembered the words, and I said I did. So she said, if I wanted to, I could put them up on the kitchen bulletin board. IMAGINE! !

"In answer to your question, yes, it's been a little better around here. Mostly because I hollered until we put up a list of jobs for everybody to do. It went like always at first, the brats goofing off, naturally. But when Mom came home and found the red check mark that meant they HADN'T made their beds or picked up the revolting garbagey living room, what do you THINK? She locked their bike in the garage!

"Honestly, I thought I'd died and gone to heaven. It was worth all the utterly ghastly screeching around here. She made a point! To help ME!

"I'll save the best till last. I still have trouble believing what she said last night. I mean, I'll believe it when it comes true, but it's something else to think she even said it.

"She was standing for a long time staring at the poster I put up. And pretty soon she said, not looking at me, that it was kind of nice, wasn't it? And I said, yes, it was.

"Then she said, still not looking at me, that you and me and her — that we'd made an awful mess of being mother and daughters. But maybe we could start over by trying to be friends.

"Well, six months ago, I would have laughed, I guess. The whole idea would have seemed just really ridiculous. But look what's happened to *us*. LIKING each other, I mean. I suppose when I got the whole cruddy routine dropped in my lap, it got through to me how you must have felt.

"Write again soon, okay? Guy and Greg laughed so hard they almost wet their pants about Frog potty-training his hamster."

Kris lay on her bed for a long time, holding the letter across her chest. Would it be possible, she wondered, for Patsy and her to teach their mother how to — well, how to walk beside them and be their friend? As well as their mother, of course. It had to be a two-way street.

Alan had once told her to try to see her mother as a human being, not just as her mother. Kris closed her eyes tight to concentrate for a moment.

Jane Wilding, Human Being. What was she? She really loved her kids, though she might never be able to tell them she did. She worked hard to keep them fed and clothed in the old house in Long Beach. It hadn't been easy for her. She admitted in the letter that she, too, had been miserable.

But *she* hadn't run away. . . . Funny she had never thought of that before.

Kris moved uneasily, considering the point, no longer as sure as she once had been that there had been no other alternative for her.

Even Chloe had told her once in her brisk way, "Honey, you can't run away from life."

Was she running away now from something else? Again, she felt the weight of her concern for Patsy, heard the despair in her sister's voice as she sobbed, ". . . nobody *cares* how I feel!"

People in a family should care about each other, should act on that caring. No wonder she had felt so rotten about leaving Patsy to cope all by herself.

Together, maybe they could make it different. Make it better for everybody? Maybe they could learn a lot, themselves, about what it took to be a family. And it sounded as though her mother might be taking the first faltering steps toward the place where they would meet her halfway.

Now there was Regan, too. He helped to make her life happier.

Kris felt the smile working its way up through her whole body till it reached her mouth, a warm good feeling. Letter in her hand, she ran to the kitchen and grabbed Chloe to hug her hard.

"I've got something to tell you," she said.